The Ookees

A Wee Tale of Fantasy

Written by Jean Marie

Illustrated by Peter Rashford

ISBN 1-930252-82-X
Copyright 1998 Jean M. Pelliccia
Illustrations Copyright 1998
Peter S. Rashford

Printed in the United States of America.

All rights reserved. No one may reproduce any part of this book without written permission from the author on story and story content or illustrator for all illustrations.

Published by PageFree Publishing, Inc.
www.pagefreepublishing.com
733 Howard Street
Otsego, MI 49078

The

Ookees

CHAPTER ONE
The Beginning

Close your eyes, open your mind and believe. Believe in a place, not so far away. It is a wondrous land, with inhabitants the same as you and me, yet so different. A civilization of human beings called Ookees, who are only three inches tall. They are a society of little people who departed from the human race, as we know it many years ago. They left the worldly pressures of an ever-growing and fast changing universe, which was squeezing in all around them. They created a simple life of quiet tranquility.

Their world was now centered in a vast meadow, full of green grass spattered here and there with every color of the rainbow.

Bright colored tulips, angel-white daisies, sun-drenched buttercups, and an array of red, blue, orange, violet and indigo blossoms; all plump and over-flowing with nectar were everywhere for as far as the eye could see.

This place they called Ookee Meadow. Here, their universe revolved around respect, love, friendship and loyalty. They had a caring and forgiving attitude toward everyone around them.

North of the Meadow was the tall and picturesque Great Northern Mountains. With their vast sweep of green trees, they were outlined against a bright blue sky. They stood strong and majestic, giving the Ookees a feeling of security.

On the West Side of Ookee Meadow was the sheltering Lilac Bush with its branches reaching so very high into the sky. The width of the bush covered half of the west part of the meadow. Its lavender colored, flowering branches seemed to droop forward as though bowing with

The Ookees ~ Page 7

respect to each new day's sun.

Behind the Lilac Bush was a most iridescent, crystal clear, babbling brook. It began its flow at the base of the Great Northern Mountains, and continued southward for as far as the eye could see and farther. Its waters sparkled in the light of day, sending off streaks of sunbeams, reflecting in all directions.

To the south stood a perfect Evergreen Forest. The forest had tall, stately trees, green and proud. The trees were one of Mother Nature's most magnificent achievements. Rustic, brown pinecones dotted each tree. The dew in the early morning sun dropped ever so softly from the needles on the trees to the moss covered ground below.

The Ookees made their homes in the warm, sheltering tulip blossoms, which grew in the meadow. In the winter, the north wind sent Sol, Mr. Sun, as you know him, farther away from the meadow, causing the cold and snow to reign there. The Ookees would then make their homes in the bulbs of the tulips to stay warm until

Sol returned the following spring.

Because the Ookees never grew more than three inches tall, Mother Nature deemed it necessary to give the Ookees a little added protection against the elements around them. She bestowed upon them exceptionally brilliant colored, silver and gold gossamer wings.

CHAPTER TWO
The Children

Off in the distance, in an area quite some ways away from the boundaries of Fantasy Valley, is the town of Superior, part of the real world, as we know it. Superior is a small country town much like the ones you drive through on a Sunday afternoon ride.

Up a particular street, we see a small run down house, its crooked shutters ready to fall at the hint of the next full breeze that touches them. The sun faded blue walls are chipped and flaked. The house is much in need of a new coat of paint.

The yard of the house is dry; the ground splitting, due to the lack of rain. No water has fallen here for quite some time. Mother Nature's green has all but abandoned everything here and for miles around as well.

From inside the house voices can be heard. "Hurry, children. You don't want to be late," encourages the soft and cheerful voice of a young beautiful woman opening the door of the house.

The woman is just saying good-bye to her husband, a slim man in his late thirties. "Have a good day dear," says the woman, holding both of his hands in hers. She gives him a kiss on the cheek.

"How can I not have a good day? I finally have a job to go to after all this time of looking. It really feels good," he says with a smile of accomplishment on his face.

"I told you things would get better, didn't I? I always had faith in you," says his wife as she gives her darkly handsome husband an affectionate hug.

"I know. I know. I thank God for that faith. It was you, and the faith you have that kept us all together these past months," he replies, returning her show of affection. "It's the first Monday I've been able to look forward to in a long time."

"And well you should," his wife adds. "It's the best job you've ever had."

"I know. The folks here seem so pleasant and friendly. For the first time in a long time, I feel we have real neighbors, real friends a real home for the kids," he says with a warm smile.

Soon, the figures of two small children run through the door and down the steps. In their urgency, they almost cause an upset on the front porch.

"Hey you guys, slow down!" the man says with a chuckle. "The school isn't going anywhere."

"We know, but our friends are waiting for us already," says Joey, their ten-year-old son. He is in the fourth grade at the country elementary school.

"Bye, you guys!" shouts the boy, as he picks up his bike from the side of the porch.

"Bye, Mom. Bye, Dad," echoes the voice of his five-year-old, younger sister Becky, who had just jumped on her bike

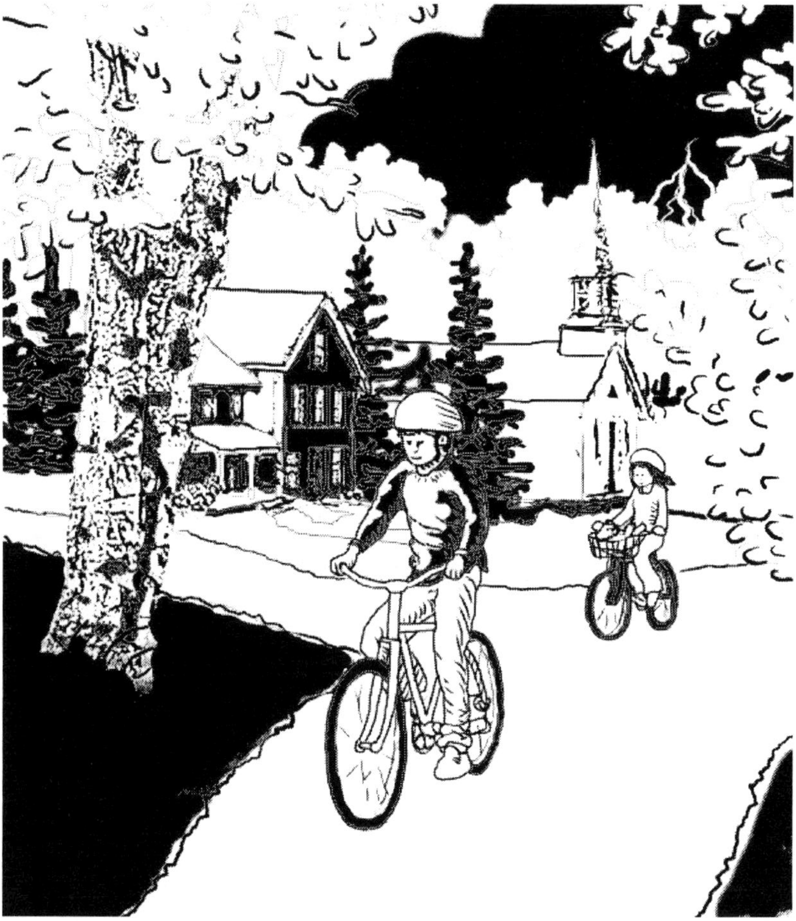

and was off in chase of her older brother.

Becky was excited at the thought of going to school and being with her friends again after a long weekend of final unpacking from their move. It had taken some time to clean, paint and repair the inside of their new house before this final unpacking could be accomplished.

The Mitchell family had moved to a new home after months of looking for work. Mr. Mitchell had lost his job. He had very little luck in finding a new job until just recently. A brand new auto plant in town had hired Mr. Mitchell; then he moved his family into the area so he could be closer to his job.

"You two be careful riding those bikes to school!" shouts the voice of their father. He worried about the two youngsters in their haste to meet their friends.

"We will, Dad. I promise," answers Joey. He waits for his sister to catch up with him. As soon as his sister has caught up, they both start to ride off, down the narrow street.

"Becky, you listen to your brother!" shouts their mother, cupping her hand to her mouth.

"I will, Mom," Becky answers.

As the children ride off in the direction of the school, Mrs. Mitchell raises her hand to shade her eyes from the brightness of the morning. She stares off into the sky.

"Just look at those clouds, dear," Mrs. Mitchell says to her husband. She stands, watching the skies above them.

"I see them!" answers her husband, as he walks down the walk of their yard. "By the looks of this yard and the rest of them in the neighborhood; we need whatever those clouds are threatening to send us."

"Yes, I agree. I hope, though, whatever the clouds are bringing; they wait until the children get to school," she says, as she watches her husband walk down the street.

Her husband disappears out of sight in the opposite direction from the one the children had just taken. Mrs. Mitchell continues to look at the sky. The town certainly needed the rain but something made her feel uneasy this morning. Something she can't explain sends cold chills throughout her body.

She rubs her crossed hands up and down her upper arms to chase away the willies. She can't shake the feeling that had grasped her only moments before. After a few more minutes of staring into space, she turns and goes inside.

Joey and Becky were hurrying to get to the next corner to be with their friends. They met their friends there each day. Then they would go to school in a group.

Today, Joey and Becky were a little later than usual. They were hoping that the others were still there. They rounded the corner. Their friends were still waiting for them.

CHAPTER THREE
On the Way to School

"Hurry Joey," called out a boy, who had red hair and freckles. He was sitting on a bike. "What took you so long, anyway? We're going to be late ifin we don't get going."

"It was Becky," Joey answered in a disgusted manor. "She had to find her dumb bear before she would leave for school."

"He's not a dumb bear, Joey. He's Pookie Bear," Becky said in her bear's defense.

"Whatever, just hurry up," Joey said to her as they joined the others.

The group headed down the street in the direction of the school. Bike after bike was headed down the street. The boy with red hair and Joey were in the lead. Becky and the others were close behind.

The wind was picking up; and it started to rain. They were peddling as fast as they could to make it to the schoolyard. They wanted to get there before they were soaked. The rain was now starting to fall quite hard.

The old covered bridge was up ahead. Once over it, they were more than half way there. Joey took the lead and the rest peddled behind him.

The wind was now blowing very hard and the rain was hitting their faces like little whips, stinging as it touched them. The rumble of thunder grew louder and more threatening. Large pellets of hail seemed to explode from the heavens. The sky was suddenly dark and black. The wind and rain were all around them.

"You guys okay back there?" Joey shouted behind him. He tried to raise his voice over the sounds of the thunder and wind, which now seemed to be surrounding them.

"Yes! Yeah! Yup!" rang out the answers of the other children, riding at a frantic pace to keep up with him.

When they finally reached the covered bridge, the water was blowing in through the cracks of the walls. A stinging spray hit them.

Joey was riding his bike near his sister Becky now, trying to keep an eye on her as the howling wind blew the rain in all directions. Suddenly, Becky stopped.

"What are you doing?" Joey cried. He whipped his bike around and headed back to where Becky was standing. He could barely see as the wind and rain whipped at his eyes.

"I dropped Pookie bear from the basket of my bike," was her reply. The other children sped by them.

"Hurry Joey," the children shouted. They passed Joey and Becky; their bikes shooting up streams of water from the now soaked bridge.

"We will!" Joey shouted after them, trying to hold his bike and grab his sister at the same time.

The wind and rain were getting worse. Joey could feel the bridge vibrating in the storm. He could see Becky struggling. She was trying to reach for her Pookie Bear that had fallen from her with one hand, while holding up her bike with the other.

"Never mind your Pookie Bear. We can come back for him later. It's raining too hard to worry about that stupid bear," Joey said, as he grabbed for her.

"No, Joey, he'll get all wet, and be scared without me," his sister replied, as she yanked away from his grasp.

Becky had just bent down to pick up Pookie Bear when the loudest clap of thunder yet roared through the sky. A lightning bolt shot down onto the roof of the old covered bridge.

RUMBLE! CRACKLE! CRASH! BANG! ZZZZ! The sounds were all around them. A gigantic lightning bolt had streaked right through the bridge roof, and then through the floor inches from where Becky was standing. It caused a large and gaping hole.

Becky screamed with fright. She had never seen anything like that before.

"You okay, Becky?" asked Joey. He was just as scared.

"I'm okay, Joey," Becky whispered her answer, swooping up her now wet bear. She started to shake from the cold and wetness now setting in.

The rain came down through the hole in torrents. The wind blew so fiercely that Becky lost her balance. As she started to fall, Joey screamed, "Becky!" He grabbed for her, but he couldn't reach her. Becky toppled over into the stream below. Instantly, without any thought, Joey jumped in behind her.

They hit the water with a huge splash. There were pieces of wood all around them from the doomed bridge. Joey grabbed the largest piece of wood near him with one hand, and Becky with the other hand.

He was still holding fast to Becky, as the rushing waters started to take them away and down stream. He never loos-

The Ookees ~ Page 22

ened his grip on her, even with the storm trying to destroy everything in its path. He was determined to not let go at any cost.

"Hang on Becky," Joey cried. He was still holding fast to the wooden board with one hand, and onto his sister with the other.

Becky couldn't answer, because the swirling waters of the stream were rushing up around her face. She was busy trying to keep her head above the rushing current, and at the same time, Becky was also holding tight to her Pookie Bear.

Joey was too busy to be scared. He knew that his sister's life depended on him holding on to her with one hand, and holding onto the board that was keeping the both of them afloat with the other. They were being swept downstream with the debris that had been washed into the fast-moving waters.

Up and down they bobbed. They turned around and around with the current's powerful force. It was like being on a giant water slide, but they had no control over when to get off. The end was no where in sight. All Joey could do was hold on and pray.

The once peaceful flowing waters of the stream were now foaming, white-water rapids. It had been very dry for a long time. The ground was too hard and dry to absorb the fast falling water. The water, the soil so desperately needed drained off into the stream instead of soaking into the ground.

The water was rushing off everywhere; falling into the waters below the town's covered bridge. The new water caused the stream to rise and surge with a wild force. These same waters were taking Joey and Becky farther and farther away.

Joey, holding tight to the board, could see the rapids ahead. They seemed to be churning and churning in a very threatening way.

"Hang on, Becky," he shouted over the loud rushing waters. "Hang on tight."

Becky didn't answer. She was too busy keeping her head up and clinging to her

Pookie Bear.

Over the rapids they went, bobbing up and down, thrashing from side to side, turning one way, and then another. For a time, Joey didn't know which way was up or down or right or left.

The devastating ride almost took the wind out of him. He just kept fighting it and fighting it. There wasn't anything else he could do.

Over the rocks they went, being thrown around like little rag dolls in a hurricane. It seemed like hours instead of minutes, that they were held in the stream's most horrible grasp.

Joey had to hold on, and also watch for debris floating by. If one of the large pieces hit him or his sister, they could be in more trouble than they already were. Joey managed to sweep Becky away from most of them, some hitting him instead.

It was a nightmare. Joey knew that if he let go of Becky, she wouldn't have a chance against the strong and violent waters of the stream. He had to hold on. He just had to.

He just couldn't fathom getting out of the water without his sister being at his side. Tired and weak, he couldn't hold on much longer. He was beginning to think that the stream, with its violent surges and lurches, would get the best of him.

Finally, the rushing waters seemed to slow down a little. Some of the thrashing and bobbing was subsiding. Joey could see things a little more clearly. Apparently, they had reached a wider part of the stream and a calming effect had begun.

Joey looked up over the board he had been grasping and could now see the shore.

"Becky, kick your feet as hard as you can. I'm going to try to swim us over to the shore."

"Okay, Joey," said a tired Becky. She was still in a state of shock. She was not aware enough of what was going on around her to be scared. She only knew she was really wet, but she was in her brother's hands.

Joey could see that they were not getting very far in their quest to get to shore. He could also see that further ahead, the stream was narrowing again and white rapids were visible once more.

"Kick harder, Becky," Joey urged. He was scared that they would be carried off again, farther than they already had been.

"I'm trying, Joey, but my legs are tired," she answered. "They don't want to work."

"I know, but try, try hard," he begged in desperation.

As the two of them kicked, Joey could see that they were not getting much closer to the shore. The power of the streams current was too strong for them to kick out of. There was not much time left before the current would pick up again, and they would be swept even further away.

"Use your free arm too!" Joey demanded. He was swimming as hard as he could with the board in one hand and Becky's hand in his other hand.

"I don't got a free arm, Joey. Pookie is in it," she said. "You have the other one," her voice was muffled; her head was bobbing in and out of the water.

"Never mind that bear. If you don't help me, none of us will ever get out of this, including the bear!" Joey said as he began to feel his body getting weaker. His legs felt numb from all the kicking in the water.

"Okay, Joey," she said. She started to paddle with her arm that held her bear.

"Swim Pookie, swim hard." She said, as she paddled with her precious Pookie Bear still tight in her hand.

Joey kicked and turned and tried to paddle through the waters of the stream for what seemed like an eternity. He was getting so tired. He could barely hold his feet up in the water to kick. They started to fall.

But what was that he felt? Was it possible? Yes, it was the bottom of the streambed. He could touch the bottom of the stream with his tiptoes. They had almost made it.

"Swim, Becky! Swim Becky, we're almost there!" he screamed to her with a new rush of strength inside him.

He was now seeing the end. It was so close. Just a few minutes more and with luck, they would be safe. He had to hold on. He had to hold on for Becky's sake as well. *Just a little further*, he thought. *Just a little way now to safety.*

Finally, holding fast to his sister, he put his feet down and could definitely feel bottom. It was the best feeling ever. He crawled up the bank of the stream. He never let loose of the board that had carried the two of them to safely, nor the hand of his sister.

As soon as he had successfully gotten them both out of the stream, he collapsed to the ground. He was gasping for air from the struggle, and his sides ached. His hand hurt from his tight grasp of the board that kept the two of them afloat.

The storm had quit as quickly as it had

begun. Becky lay beside him. She was starting to cry.

"Oh, Becky, now is not the time to cry. We're safe. Now is the time to be happy," he said to cheer her up as well as himself. At the same time, he was trying to calm her fear from the ordeal the two of them had just been through.

"I'm not crying because I'm scared, I'm crying because I almost lost Pookie bear. I love him almost as much as I love you Joey," she said with a tremble in an anguished voice.

"Well, you didn't lose the bear so you can stop crying," said Joey.

"I can't stop crying," she said, sobbing even harder.

"Why in the world not?" Joey asked, starting to get frustrated with the whole situation.

"Because Pookie Bear is all wet," she said, as she held up the drowned looking matted bear.

Pookie Bear's arms were twisted from the struggle of the swim. Pieces of grass and dirt were embedded in his long furry coat. His neck was stretched out. He looked as if a freight train had run him over. The look on his face, along with his bright red smile, gave the bear the look of a clown.

If the situation were not what it was, Joey would be rolling in the grass dying with laughter at the sight of the soaking wet and out of shape bear. As it was, he knew he had to calm his sister.

"He'll dry. He'll dry," said Joey, almost unable to control his laughter. They could have been hurt or even killed, and all his sister could worry about is her wet, stupid bear.

Becky was beginning to cry even more. "Now, what's the matter with you? I told you that your bear would dry, didn't I?"

"I'm not crying because of that, Joey," she answered in a whining voice.

"Oh brother, then why are you crying now?"

"Because you're mad at Pookie and

me for nearly getting us drownedid," she answered.

Joey realized that his sister was still in the state of shock, and knew he had to calm her down from being so afraid.

"I'm not mad at you or Pookie Bear, Becky, but I will be if you don't stop crying."

He bent over and gave her a hug and peck on the cheek to convince her he was not angry with her. Becky looked up at her brother and smiled as she held up her bear to him.

"What?" Joey asked as the bear was within a couple of inches of his face.

"Give Pookie Bear a kiss, too, so he knows you're not mad at him either," she said as if that would make everything better.

Joey started to say something and then stopped. He knew that one small kiss could solve his problem with his little sister. He reluctantly gave the Pookie Bear a peck on the head. Boy, he thought. It was a good thing his friends were not there to see that.

It had been worth it though, for it seemed to calm his sister down. She was now, lying beside him, resting and gathering her strength back. She seemed to be getting back to her old self again.

After a few minutes of rest, Joey got up and was helping Becky get to her feet.

"Come on, Becky. The rain is stopping and we better get to school before everyone starts to worry about us," he told her as he started to walk in the direction he thought would be toward the school.

"Okay, Joey," she responded. "Come on, Pookie. We gotta get to school now. We're already late."

She brushed the grass off of Pookie Bear and was ready. She smiled at Joey, and held her hand up for him to grasp. They were on their way.

But how could Joey know that the stream had washed them far away from their original destination. With the stream's twists, turns and bends, they were now headed in a completely different direction than that of their school.

CHAPTER FOUR
A Search for the Children

Meanwhile, back at the little run down house that had been so happy just a few hours before, the Sheriff was knocking at the door. He had a worried look on his face.

"Mrs. Mitchell?" he asked as Becky and Joey's mother answered the door.

"Yes, what is it?" she asked in a frightened tone.

"Is Mr. Mitchell here with you?" he asked.

"Why, no, he's working down at the plant on the other side of town. Why do you ask? What's going on?"

"May my deputy and I come in for a few minutes? I'd like to talk to you," he asked.

"Yes, of course, come on in," she said,

almost afraid of what he was about to say.

As the Sheriff and his deputy sat down in the living room, Mrs. Mitchell was getting more and more scared.

"Is it the children? Has something happened to my children?" she asked, her hands starting to shake.

"Then, I presume that they didn't come back home?" the sheriff replied.

"No, why would they come home? They just left for school only a few hours ago."

"That's why we are here, Mrs. Mitchell. Your two kids never made it to school. The children they usually ride to school with said that there was an accident on the bridge. One of the boys said that lightning had hit the bridge and that your children were on the bridge when it hit."

"When Becky and Joey didn't show up at school right away, the children figured that they came home instead of continuing to school. When the teachers found out what had happened, they had the school call the Sheriff's Office. I, in turn, had hoped to find Becky and Joey had come back here and was safe, but it seems that they did not."

"What does this mean? Do you think that my children are drowned?" She could say no more. She was completely overcome by the thought of her children being lost to her forever.

"Calm down, Mrs. Mitchell," the Sheriff said as he tried to comfort her. "I don't think anything of the sort. They may have been washed away in the stream under the covered bridge," he said. "If that's the case, we'll find them."

He could tell that Mrs. Mitchell was paying no attention to him at all. She was in a state of shock and quite beside herself with worry. He got up and motioned for his deputy to follow him to the front door.

"Get out to the car and radio our office, and the State Police," he ordered the deputy. "Have them call out a search party, and also send a car to the plant to alert Mr. Mitchell of the children's disappearance. We'll all meet at the covered bridge within the hour."

The fire siren in the town's fire barn was going off; the church bells from every church in town were ringing. The entire town knew then that something was dreadfully wrong, and that they should assemble at the town square.

Soon, people from all directions were assembling in the middle of town. The entire community immediately organized an all out search. The whole town was concerned. The entire search party gathered together. They went looking for the two children who had last been seen on the bridge before the lightning hit.

Mr. Mitchell had been alerted to the fact that his children were missing. He immediately left the factory. He joined in the search, while some of the women of the town went to comfort his wife at their home. As much as she wanted to aid in the search, Mrs. Mitchell was hoping that there was still a chance the children would find their way home. She wanted to be there, if they did. She had to stay there and wait, wait and pray.

CHAPTER FIVE
The Land of the Ookees

While the search was going on, the children were still trying to find the school.

"This seems like an awful long way to school, Joey. I'm getting pooped," said a very tired Becky. "Let's rest for a few minutes."

Joey knew that they had gone entirely too far to be anywhere near the school, but he didn't want to worry his sister.

"No, we can't rest now, Becky," he responded. "We're just beginning to have some fun. I thought that this would be like an adventure for us. We could take the long way around, and enjoy the walk through the woods."

"But Joey, I thought you said that we had to hurry so everyone wouldn't worry about us?"

"Well, I did say that, but we'll get there soon enough. Why all of a sudden, do you seem to remember everything I say? If I wanted you to remember something you wouldn't."

"I don't know, Joey, but I wish we were at school now."

"We'll get there and as I said, it'll be soon enough."

"What's that mean, soon enough?" asked Becky. She was getting quite tired from all the walking, as well as being bored with the situation.

"It means just that, soon enough," Joey replied, for the lack of a better answer.

"You mean we're lost?" said Becky, surprising Joey with her awareness of their circumstances.

"Well, yes," Joey replied. "But it's still an adventure."

Becky smiled up at her brother, and again gave him her hand. His total calmness put her at ease. Her confidence in her brother was very strong. As she looked at it, if he wasn't worried, there was nothing to worry about.

The two of them continued on the path they were on. Becky was enjoying the frolicking of the small forest animals that lined the path. It was truly wonderful.

The squirrels and chipmunks were busy gathering food and playing from tree to tree. They would chase each other now and then, trying to take the others bounty of nuts. They moved so fast, that it made Becky laugh. In the distance, a deer could be seen, its head adorned with the largest rack of any deer she had ever come upon in any zoo.

"Look!" Becky shouted with excitement to her brother Joey. She pointed to where the magnificent male deer was grazing.

Before Joey had the chance to respond to his sister's wishes, the deer heard her and vanished in an instant.

"Oh, he's gone," said Becky, disappointed.

"What's gone, Becky? Who's he?"

"Bambie's dad, that's who *he* is," Becky said with her head down.

"Well, Bambie's dad is gone, because you startled him. Remember Dad telling us that if we see an animal in the forest, we had to be really quiet so we didn't scare it away?"

"Ya, I remember, but it's too late now. He's gone."

"Well, he's not the only deer in the forest. Maybe we will see more and this time, we'll be quiet so they won't run away, okay?" Joey said to cheer her up.

"Okay, Joey," she replied smiling. He had managed to comfort her again.

The children and their parents had lived for most of their lives in the city. They had only saw animals in the confinement of a zoo. Here, where they were free, they seemed somehow different from the ones they saw in the cages of the zoo. They seemed to have more energy and life in them as they moved around in the woods.

But now, Becky was starting to get hungry. It had been a long time since breakfast.

"Joey, I'm hungry," said Becky in a matter of fact way.

"I know, me too," he said.

Joey looked off the path and saw some familiar berries. He had seen the same berries in the woods behind their house. His father had pointed them out about a week ago, when they had been out exploring the wonders of Mother Nature.

"Here, Becky, eat some of these," he said, as he handed her some of the freshly picked berries.

"Where do I wash my hands, Joey? Mom says to always wash our hands before we eat."

"There is no place to wash, Becky. Just eat the berries."

"Okay, Joey, but mom's gonna be mad," she answered as she began to eat her lunch.

Joey couldn't help but smile over what she had said. Mom would have more serious things on her mind with them being gone so long, than the fact that they had not washed their hands before they ate their berries. They ate the berries until their stomachs were satisfied.

"Come on Becky," ordered Joey as he stood up. "Let's get going."

"Okay," she replied, as she stood beside him. "Are we going home now?"

"We're gonna try," he answered her, hoping home was not far away.

Joey continued to search for landmarks that looked even the least bit familiar. They had walked for quite a while without finding anything that meant they were any closer to home.

Soon, they came to a large thicket. It seemed to stretch out as far as they could see in either direction.

"Can we go over there and pick some flowers?" Becky asked.

She looked across the thicket to the meadow on the other side. On the right was the tallest mountain Becky had ever seen. On the left was a green forest of trees and between the two, a large field of tulips, in bright rainbow colors.

The Ookees ~ Page 45

"I guess we could," Joey said. "I can't see any harm in stopping for just a few minutes. We'll have to find a way through all these bushes first though."

"Okay, and I'll help. Won't mom love the flowers we bring her, Joey?" Becky said, as she started to run along side the thicket, trying to find a way through to the beautiful garden on the other side.

The two of them seemed to walk forever, still not finding a way through the large thicket. It went on and on. There was not even the slightest path for them to go through.

"I don't think we are going to find a way through these bushes, Becky," Joey said, as he looked all around them.

"Can't we crawl through them then?" She asked. "There's a hole back here. Maybe we could get through that way."

"Where?" Joey asked.

"Come on, Pookie and I will show you," Becky said, as she ran back to where she had seen the opening just minutes before.

Joey followed Becky to where she had spotted a small separation in the thicket's tightly gnarled branches.

"See, right here," Becky said, as she pointed to the spot.

"I, ah, don't know about that Becky," Joey replied. He was hesitant to take her through the thickly webbed branches.

"Why not, Joey? You said this was an as...ben...ture, didn't you?"

Joey laughed at his sister's attempt in trying to pronounce the big word. "Oh, all right, but you follow me and stay close, you hear?" he ordered.

"Okay, I will, I promise," answered Becky, joyfully.

"Let's put your hair under your shirt so it won't get tangled up in the branches," Joey said, as he started to tuck her long curls under her shirt and down her back.

"That's good enough, Joey," she said, anxious to get started.

"Ready?" He asked her.

"Ready, Joey," she replied.

"Okay, give me Pookie Bear," he said.

"No, I'm taking him with me."

"Okay, then let's go."

Joey bent down and led the way into the small thicket opening. Becky took Pookie Bear with her. She wanted to share with him this wild adventure. Becky had no idea the real adventure would begin on the other side of the thicket. An adventure they would remember for the rest of their lives.

It seemed to take forever for them to reach the other side. The further they went the more trouble they had. Every time they touched a branch or rubbed up against one, dust would rain down all over them. It was not your normal type of dust. This dust was all shiny and twinkled in the sunlight blazing through the branches of the thicket. The further they went, the more tired they became. It was beginning to be a struggle to put one hand in front of the other.

The sparkle dust was falling down all over them. More and more fell as they crept through the thicket. The shimmering effects made by the dust made it difficult to see.

Soon, Joey could see an opening in front of them.

"I can see the other side, Becky. We're almost there," he called back to her.

"I hope so. I'm getting awfully tired, Joey," she said, trying not to yawn.

"I know, but stay awake. We're almost there," he coaxed.

"I don't know if I can. I'm so sleepy," she said. "Pookie Bear is too. Aren't you Pookie?"

"Yes, you can, Becky. Remember that this is an adventure. You have to keep going, or Pookie Bear won't see the adventure."

Joey was worried about Becky. He, too, was getting tired. He just wanted to get out of the thicket with her. He had to keep her going for just a little while longer.

Soon, his fears were put to rest. He had made it out the other side. It felt good to stand up again. Joey was still a little dizzy from the trip through the thicket.

He bent down to help Becky get out

of the thicket. He pulled on her until she was completely free from its branches. She was now asleep on the ground, still clutching her faded, damp, and tattered Pookie Bear.

"Becky," he yawned. "Wake up. We made it through."

By now, Joey could barely keep his eyes opened. He knelt down beside Becky, and tried even harder to wake her up.

"Wake up Becky," he said, as he shook her shoulder. "Now is not the time to go to sleep. There are the tulips you wanted to see. Please, Becky, wake up. Wake up."

Becky stirred, but only long enough to open one eye, smile, and clasp her Pookie to her chest.

Joey couldn't keep his eyes open any more. He gently dropped beside his sister on the soft green grass of the meadow. Almost instantly, he too, fell sound asleep.

CHAPTER SIX
The Meadow Land

A quiet breeze was blowing. The two children slept deeply on the cool, green grass of the meadow. The sun was sending down rays. They bounced off them every which way. Its beams were dancing off the dust now floating around Joey and Becky as they slept. The sparkling dust covering their head and bodies seemed to be pulling the sun's light all around them. It was an eerie sight, and yet it was one of calm and beauty.

In the meadow, quite close to where the children were sleeping, there were little sounds. The tall grass was moving ever so slightly. The little sounds became whispers. The whispers were changing to mumbles and finally to words. Something was talking ever so quietly.

"Do you think they are asleep?"

"I'm not sure."

"Has it been long enough yet?"

"Don't know."

"I wonder what they are?"

"I have no idea."

A soft rumble of many different little voices surrounded Becky and Joey as they slept.

"They're not Ookees. They're too big."

"That's right. They haven't any wings either."

"Maybe their wings fell off already."

"Nah, it's too early in the year."

"Stay away from them; I tell you. They're trouble."

"Oh, hush up now. How do you know?"

"They're from the outside world, aren't they? They are not one of us, are they? They don't belong here, do they? That's all I have to know."

"Oh, just hush."

There were a few moments of silence before anyone else said a thing.

"I think they're children," said a lady's

soft voice. The tiny beings of the Meadow started to emerge from the tall grass. They walked between the blades of grass. One at a time they showed their presence at the meadow's edge.

The little ones that came into view were merely three inches tall, but they still had many human characteristics. Their simple clothes swayed in the breezes of the meadow.

Their hair, some long and some short, some light colored and some darker, was being swirled about by the gentle winds that blew there. Their silver and gold wings glistened as the sun shown upon them. There were men and women, and they were creeping closer and closer to the sleeping children.

"What makes you think they are children?"

"Because of this one," she pointed to Becky. As the others looked, the smaller of the two strangers could be seen cuddling a stuffed animal in its arms.

"Upon closer examination of these

creatures from the outside world, I find that one is a very young girl and the other is a slightly older boy," said one of the male beings with great authority.

"How do you know that?"

"Look at their hair, and the clothes they are wearing. Yep, I say one boy and one girl. Kids, that's what we have here."

"Children, how wonderful," said an Ookee woman.

Yes, the children had penetrated the boundaries of Fantasy Valley. They had entered a place where there were no other humans of their size. They had entered the world of the Ookees.

"Harrumph, children or not, don't get any ideas. They're still outsiders," spoke the strong male voice of an older Ookee with a white beard.

"Yes, siree, they're still outsiders. We've gotta do what we got to do," uttered the same Ookee. He seemed to have an inner fear of outsiders. "We better do something mighty quick, too."

"Maybe so, but they are still children.

We can't just leave them here indefinitely," added one of the other women.

"What do you say, King Baldwin?"

The King just stood in silence, studying the situation over and over.

"First, run back to the village and bring back some ropes, ladders and some pulleys," he ordered.

As some of the Ookees ran to do the King's bidding, the rest stood watch over the children. These were strangers; who had entered their peaceful valley without invitation.

Soon, the others had returned with the things that the King requested.

"What now, Sire?" the Ookees asked with ladders in hand.

"Now, I say we brush the angel dust from their faces and hair and let them wake up. We'll talk with them before we decide to do anything more," replied the King.

"Yes, Sire," the Ookees replied.

The King motioned for the Ookees to do as he had recommended. The tiny beings swiftly ran to where the children were lying sound to sleep on the ground before them. They quickly raised themselves up the children's bodies by ladders, ropes and large pulleys.

Standing on the children's shoulders on their tiptoes, the women worked to clear the angel dust from the children's faces. The men, hanging from the ropes and pulleys, cleared the dust away from their hair.

"*Kerchooo.*" A sneeze rang out. "*Kerchooo! Kerchooo!*" The angel dust was floating all around them, causing them to sneeze and sneeze.

"Remember, just their faces and heads, and no more," King Baldwin reminded them.

"Yes, Sire," was their response in unison.

Soon they were finished. They went back to the tall grass of the Meadow taking their ladders, ropes and pulleys with them. Then they waited for the children to awaken from their sleep.

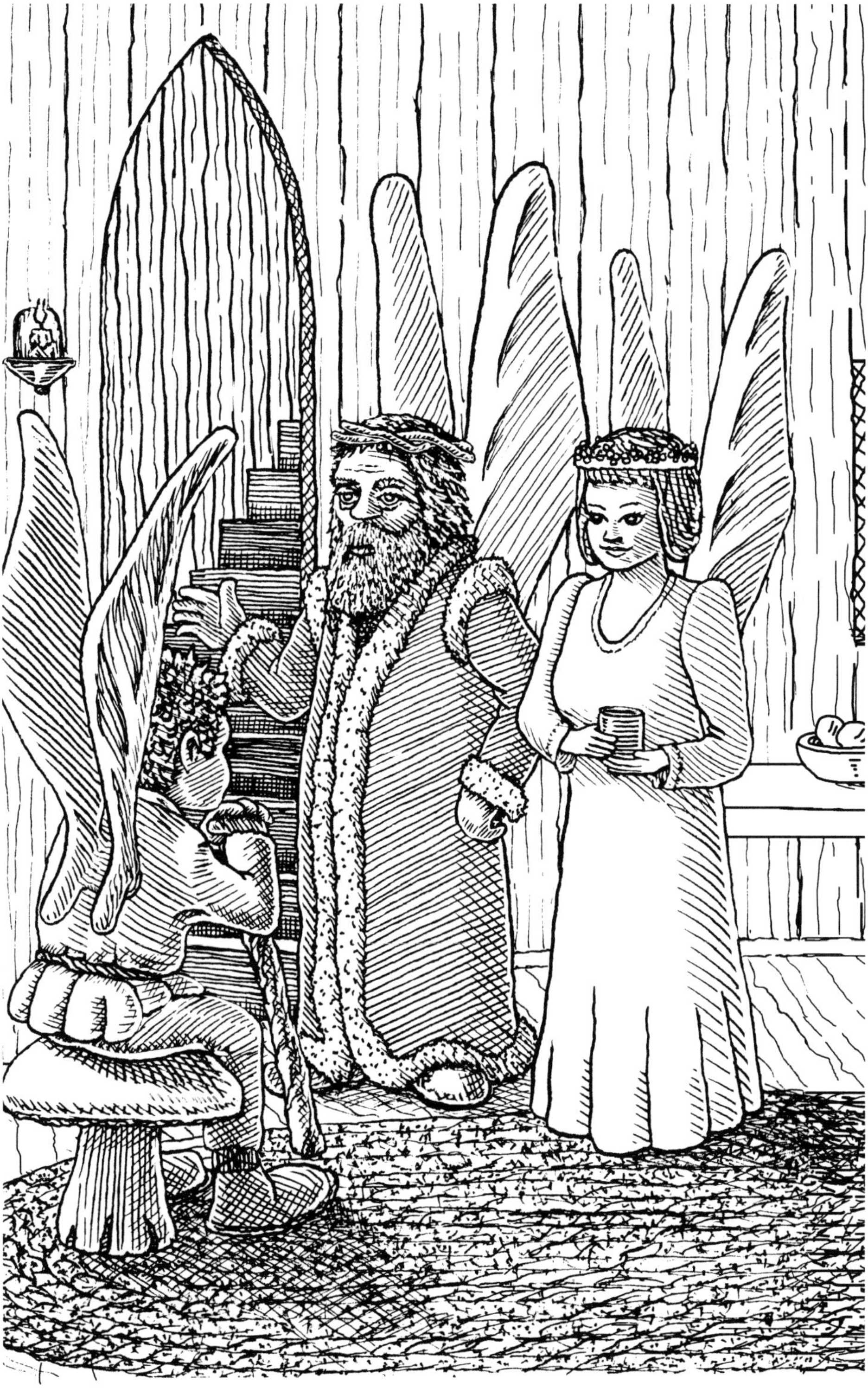

It wasn't long before the children started to stir. They would now be able to move their heads and speak, but that was all. The rest of their body was still covered with the angel dust, causing a completely, paralyzing effect.

Joey was the first to come to his senses. He opened his eyes and began to look around. He seemed to be struggling. His body would not move. It was very frustrating for him. What was wrong? Why couldn't he move? How could he protect and care for Becky, if he couldn't move? Maybe he was still asleep and only dreaming.

That was it, he was still asleep. He and his sister had been through a lot. They had been extremely tired when they fell asleep. I'm only dreaming; he thought as he lay there. He started to close his eyes again.

"It will do you no good to try to move, for it is impossible. You are under our spell. We mean you no harm. We just want to know what the two of you are doing here,"

King Baldwin said, with a lot of suspicion in his voice.

Joey quickly opened his eyes again. He knew now, as he listened to that strange voice, that he was no longer dreaming.

"Who are you? Where are you? Why can't I see you?" Joey questioned."

"If you look this way, you can see me," answered a voice. It sounded as if it were coming from over his right shoulder.

As Joey moved his eyes in that direction, he saw something that was totally amazing. He had never experienced anything like it before. His eyes followed, as an exceptionally small being started to walk across his shoulders and onto his chest.

"Why are you so small? What happened to us?" Joey questioned in disbelief.

"Never mind about me," the King said gruffly. "Why are you here in our Meadow?" the King repeated, even more firmly.

Joey was now getting scared. He was scared for himself as well as for his sister who was just starting to wake up. He was scared of the thought of someone having the power to keep someone else from moving; someone so small having this kind of power over him. He was so much larger than they were. What else might these people be able to do to them? He decided to answer the questions being asked of him, in order to give him more time to think over the situation.

"We were on our way to school, riding our bikes with all our friends. The storm came up and destroyed the bridge. We fell into the water, floated downstream, got out of the water and that's all. We were just walking. We didn't hurt anything. Why are you doing this to us?" Joey replied hesitantly.

"We are doing nothing to you except keeping you down until we get to the truth. You just be nice and still."

"But, that is the truth, I swear. We fell into the stream and were washed away in the storm. We finally managed to make it to shore and were just heading back to school when we came to the thicket. Please let us go. Becky is waking up, and she will need me."

Becky was now quite awake. She was confused. She couldn't understand why she couldn't get up.

"Joeeey, Joeeey," she called, starting to cry.

"I'm here, Becky. It's okay. Ah, ah, ah, don't you like this game?" He asked her, trying to keep her calm.

"What game Joey? Why can't I move? What's happening, Joey? I'm scared," she said, as she started to cry again. She was still straining to get up.

"No, Becky, don't be scared. It's okay, I'm here," Joey said to her, not knowing what else to do.

"I don't like it Joey. I don't want to play this game anymore. Make it stop, please Joey, make it stop," Becky begged as she continued to cry even harder.

Becky was struggling so hard to move

and get up, but she couldn't. She was becoming very frightened. Joey felt more helpless than before. He could do nothing to calm her fears. He too, began to struggle even harder than before for lack of not knowing anything else to do.

"That's enough. This is going to stop and right now," spoke the angry voice of Queen Rameena, Baldwin's wife.

She came out of the tall grass and called to Becky.

"Becky, Becky, over here, Becky. Can you see me over here?" asked the Queen.

Becky's cries calmed a little when she heard the soft voice of a woman calling to her. She tried to focus through her tears, in the direction of the soft voice that was calling her name.

"I think I can see you. You look so small."

"That is because I am small. Much smaller than you," answered the Queen.

"Can you help me?" Becky asked, as she sobbed the words. "I can't move."

"Of course, dear, we will all help you." the Queen said as she motioned for the swered the King, looking straight into his wife's eyes.

"You must understand that. I have the entire meadow's interests to think about. If we let them go, and they hurt even one of us; there is nothing any of us can do."

"I do understand that, but we have the dust pellets that Mother Nature gave us in case of such an emergency. Some of our best shooters can stand ready in the bushes behind the children. At the first and slightest sign of trouble, they can bombard them with the pellets. They will be as harmless and non-threatening as they are now. Besides, he has such compassion for his sister; I think he will do whatever we say in order to take her fear from her."

King Baldwin thought over what his wife had said for quite some time, before he spoke again.

"If we release you, and allow you to move a little more freely; will you promise to stay where you are?" asked the King.

rest of the Ookees to come and help.

"Can you please help my brother, Joey, too?" She asked.

"Yes, dear, we'll help Joey too."

The Ookees stared first at King Baldwin, and then back to Queen Rameena. The King had said that the magic dust should be removed only from their faces and hair. The Queen was now ordering them to wipe off the rest of the magic dust and fully release their hostages from their spell. The little people were confused at the conflicting orders of the royal pair.

King Baldwin stood fast and said nothing. Queen Rameena saw that it was a stand off between letting the children go and leaving them as they were.

"Becky, lie still and I'll be right back, okay?" the Queen said as she turned and walked back in the direction of her husband and King.

"Baldwin, they are scared, especially the little girl. We just can't let them lie there so frightened."

"Don't you think I realize that?" an

"Yes, we promise," answered Joey. "Only help Becky first, please."

King Baldwin hesitated for a moment. He stared at his beloved wife, Rameena. She had always been an excellent judge of character. He looked towards his subjects, and gave his nod of approval.

He knew that either he or his wife would have to give in. In this case, he trusted the instincts of his wife. All of the Ookees came from their hiding places. They began to wipe away the angel dust that was placing the spell over the children.

"Don't move Becky. Be real quiet until I say to move, okay?" Joey said tenderly.

"Remember; wait until I tell you it's all right.

"Okay, Joey, I won't move," Becky replied.

"Don't you move either, Pookie."

Becky was completely enthralled with all that was happening. There were Ookees everywhere, wiping and dusting her, as if she was a piece of her mother's furniture. She couldn't believe what she saw.

"Hee, hee, hee, hee!" Becky laughed. "You're tickling my neck."

"Hee, hee, hee, hee!" rang out the returned laughter from the Ookee women who were brushing Becky off.

Soon, it was all wiped away. The Ookees fearfully ran back behind the King and Queen. They were waiting to see what would happen next.

When the Ookees had all gone, and no sounds were heard for some time; Joey lifted his head and looked in the direction where the King and Queen were standing.

"Can we get up now?" asked Joey.

"Of course you can," the King answered. "The dust has been removed."

Joey started to sit up carefully, watching to see that none of the Ookees were close enough that he might squash them. He kept looking all around him. On his hands and knees, he felt the grass. Then he stood up slowly, making sure there were no tiny beings under him he might accidentally hurt.

The Ookees stood back in awe and shock over the size of the boy who was now standing before them. He completely towered over the Ookees, the bushes, and the thicket of the meadow.

He bent down again and crawled over to Becky. Using the same caution, he helped her to sit up. He then sat down beside her in the soft grass of the meadow. He reached for her, and brought her up to sit in front of him.

"Now stay right here, Becky. There are hundreds of little people everywhere. You might step on one of them, if you move too quickly."

"Okay, Joey, I won't move. I promise," she answered with a smile. She was completely confident in her brother's sheltering arms.

"Now, we have shown you; that we mean you no harm," began the King. "It is your turn to do the same for us, and tell us why you have trespassed into the realm of our Meadow."

Joey sat close to his sister. He began to explain to the Ookees the whole reason; they were in the Meadow in the first place.

"...And that is the whole truth. Honest it is," explained Joey. "Becky just wanted to pick some flowers for our mother."

"Yup, that is the whole trooff," repeated Becky. "If you don't believe us, you can ask Pookie Bear," she said, as she smiled and held up her bear for all to see.

Some of the Ookees started to laugh. Some were quite shocked at the thought of someone coming into their village, and chopping down their flower homes.

The royal couple had to make a decision about what to do with the children of the outside world. Even though they were not Ookees, they were children who needed to be helped.

King Baldwin and Queen Rameena stood staring at the children, and then at each other.

"We must go back to the village and discuss this situation amongst ourselves. Can we trust you to both stay here, and not enter the Meadow any further than you already have?" asked the King.

"Yes, sir, you can," answered Joey.

"Come," King Baldwin motioned to the rest of the Ookees. "There are chores to be done."

"May I stay here, father, and visit with the strangers?" asked his daughter, the Princess Tatashee.

The Princess was just as awed by Becky, as Becky was by her. She was a very inquisitive Ookee. She loved learning new and different things. This was surely a new and different thing to study and learn about, giants from another world.

"Only if two of the guards, with tranquilizer pellets, stay with you; and you stay out of the way of the children," answered her mother, before her father had a chance to say no.

King Baldwin was usually very strict with

his daughter. She had very little freedoms compared to the other village maidens of her age.

Queen Rameena knew by the tenderness and compassion Joey showed for his sister, the Princess would be safe with them.

Queen Rameena, King Baldwin, and the other Ookees left. The

Princess and two of the guards stayed behind with the children. They headed back to their village. They had to discuss what they could do with Joey and Becky.

CHAPTER SEVEN
Ookee Life

The rest of the Ookees left, but the Princess and the guards stayed behind. The Princess Tatashee remained a safe distance away from the children. The guards, with the tranquilizing pellets, remained in the branches over their heads, awaiting any trouble.

"Are you really a princess?" asked Becky.

"Yes, I am, Becky."

"Where is your castle?" Becky added.

"Right over there," the Princess pointed toward the tulips.

"Over there, Princess?" Becky asked confused. "But I don't see any castle. All I see are tulips."

"That's right, Becky. See the large bouquet in the center of the tulips?"

Tatashee asked.

"You mean the white ones?" Becky asked. "The ones right in the middle of all of them?"

"Yes, those are the ones. That is my castle. I live there with my father and mother. All the tulips that you see there are our homes. Together, they form our Village, Ookee Village."

"Could you tell us more about your people?" asked Joey.

"Sure, I can tell you everything you want to know," said the Princess. She began her story. The guards were still very close by. They were concentrating on any sudden move by the children.

She told them that her people were the Ookees. For nearly a hundred years, they had been a peaceful and loving group of people. They were always thinking of the needs of their neighbors, especially the older folks, or those without families. They were always there for the sick or poorer members of the Valley who had hard times providing for their families, especially during the cold winter months and the holiday seasons.

All were well-educated and very religious. The Ookees got along very well with each other, and with the other beings of the Meadow. They were always so tolerant of the different customs, traditions and ways of life that were shared there. Although they were very bright, the Ookees didn't know about the outside world.

They were very industrious and worked hard at their chores and duties in the village. They spent their days gathering nectar, which was part of their food supply, from the flowers and blossoms of the Meadow.

The webs from their friends, the spiders, and the threads from the silkworms were woven into cloth. This cloth was used to make clothes and linens.

Some Ookees would collect different colored berries. These were used as dye to lightly color the delicate strands, before they were woven into useful materials.

Others busied themselves construct-

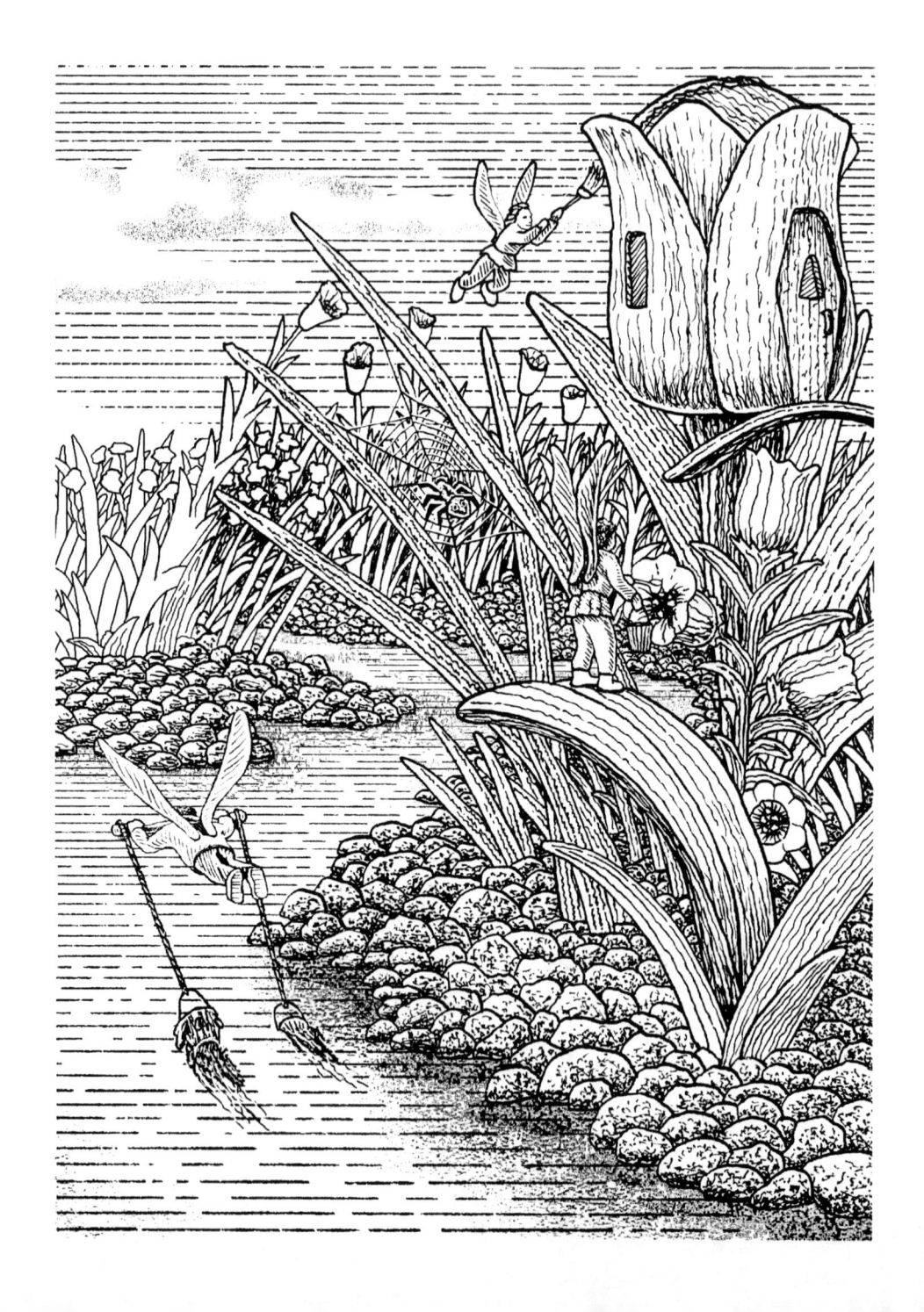

The Ookees ~ Page 74

ing some of the other things that made life more comfortable for the Ookees. Along with their daily chores, they were all responsible for keeping the Meadow neat and tidy. They kept their tulip homes clean, beautiful to look at, and pleasant to live in. When their work was done, Ookees could be found laughing and singing. They also played games among the flowers. Playing games is what they liked doing most of all.

    Everyone had a job to do in Ookee Valley. Ookee Valley was divided into the Village where the Ookees lived, and the Meadow where they worked and played.

    "My mother and father, King Baldwin and Queen Rameena are the rulers of our people," the Princess went on to explain. "The two of you met them a few minutes ago, remember?" asked Tatashee.

    The children nodded. They were deep in thought. They were thinking about the story they were hearing.

    The Princess continued with the story. She began to describe her parents to the children.

"Please don't think that my father is mean or uncaring, because that is far from the truth. I often hear my father pacing the floors of our castle, night after night. He is either worrying about something, or trying to figure out new ways of making things easier or more enjoyable for his subjects.

"He is the most caring and sympathetic person I know; but he has a hard time showing it. Once you get to know him better, you will understand what I mean. Let's put it this way, if someone has a problem, he thinks of it as his problem. If one of us is hurting, he too, is hurting. Any ill affect on anything or anyone in the meadow affects him."

"To put it all in a nutshell, he carries the whole Valley on his shoulders at times. Do you understand what I am trying to say?" She asked the children.

"Yes, I think I do," answered Joey, really thinking about what the Princess had said. Becky just nodded in agreement.

She went on to tell them that her father was a dedicated and powerful king. He stood two spider webs taller than the other Ookees. Always, he would stand before them strong and stately. He spoke with confidence security.

He usually dressed in a robe of spider web and rabbit fur. The robe was dyed royal blue and burgundy by berry juices. His powerful gold wings lay straight and strong on his back. His crown made of grapevines, dried berries, and pinecone seeds, emphasized his royal image as King.

"That was him all right," interrupted Joey. "I sure could tell he was a King by the way he looked and talked. Everyone else listened."

Tatashee and the guards smiled as their story continued. She went on to describe her mother to them. Her mother was a subject she loved to talk about. She was very close to her.

Queen Rameena shared the King's lofty ideals about life in the Meadow. Unlike King Baldwin, however, she showed a much more sensitive approach to the every day needs of her subjects. The King would always hide his feelings.

Queen Rameena stood an acorn cap shorter than the King did. She dressed in spider web and silk threaded garments. The juices of the apple blossom and lilac petals swirled beautiful colors of lavender and pink throughout her wispy, shimmering gown. Her shoes, made of apple blossom petals, were wrapped delicately around her feet. They were laced with pink silk thread. The Queen's wings lay daintily upon her shoulders. Her crown, a ring of ivy with forget-me-nots and baby's breath, encircled her silvery, shoulder-length hair.

She, too, had much love for the Ookees she ruled over, and spent a lot of time listening to their individual problems and sharing in their happiness.

Baldwin and Rameena were good and sensible rulers who treated their subjects, all the Meadow Ookees, very kindly. In turn, the Ookees loved and honored their chosen King and Queen.

For as long as anyone could remember, King Baldwin's family had ruled over Ookee Valley. In the past, the first born had always been a son. It was that son, who took on the rule of the Meadow and Village, when it was time for his Parents to step down. King Baldwin and Rameena's first born and only child was a daughter. She would eventually rule the lands of the Ookees, when her father and mother were no longer able to reign as King and Queen.

"I think that most of all, we Ookees love Princess Tatashee," explained the guards, speaking highly of the now blushing Princess. Both guards smiled affectionately at the Princess as the story continued.

It was easy to see why the Ookees were so fond of their Princess. She was not only kind and wise, but the most beautiful of all the Ookees. She had dainty wings of bright, sparkling silver and long golden hair that shone like rays of sunlight. As she glided through her daily chores, her gown would blow softly in the gentle breezes. Her slippers, of soft yellow buttercup petals, matched the glimmer of yellows and greens that cascaded through her gown. Her crown was of golden rod. It sparkled with angel flakes. It was a gift befitting a Princess, given to her by Mother Nature, at her royal birth.

Princess Tatashee, like her parents, was gentle and loving. She was very humble, even though she was a Princess, and was adored by her subjects.

The Princess had greatly impressed Becky and had won her trust, but Joey was another story. He was still quite skeptical of her and the other Ookees. He was deep in thought, wondering about the fate that would eventually await him and Becky.

The Princess hoped that by the time she was through explaining their world she would gain Joey's trust as well.

It was important for the Ookees to gain the friendship, respect, and trust of both children. It might be a long time before they could find a way to get the children home again. The Ookees knew that if the children trusted and respected them, they would listen to what they were told and believe in what was said. In this way, the children would be safe from harm with the Ookees, until they could get back to their own home. The Ookees needed the children to do exactly as they said so that no harm would come to anyone of the Valley while the children were waiting to leave. Trust and respect for each other was essential for both sides to survive. There might be a long time of being together, before a solution was found to get the children home safely again.

Life was very good for the Ookees. They owned little of any real value, only what they needed, to live happy and contented lives. There were more than enough flowers and blossoms in the meadow to supply nectar for them to eat. When they were thirsty, they quenched their thirst at the crystal-clear, spring-fed stream that babbled alongside the Meadow. Thus all their real needs were met.

CHAPTER EIGHT
The Lugaluks

The world that the Ookees lived in was as perfect as it could be, except for one thing, the Lugaluks.

The Lugaluks were cruel, heartless and warlike dragonflies. They lived in the nearby Swamp, just the other side of the Evergreen Forest. Their surroundings, unlike the Meadow, were dark and foreboding. They seemed to like it that way.

The Princes explained the Lugaluks and the differences between them and the Ookees. Joey's eyes opened wide. He was intrigued with the Dragonfly's story.

Now, they had his attention. He began to understand that the Ookees too, had their share of problems. Being older than his sister, he couldn't relate to the Ookees with all their goodness and perfection. He knew that with all that bliss and happiness; there would be something to upset things.

Even at his young age, he realized that goodness could only be felt and realized by having something to relate it to. He knew that the Ookees could realize the goodness in themselves, when they had the meanness of the Lugaluks to measure it up to.

As the story continued, Joey was enthralled with what he was hearing. The dragonfly's homes were all in the base of he trees growing in the dark, murky waters of the Swamp. Only creatures like the Lugaluks cared to live there. They were evil and nasty creatures. The Ookees were glad that the Evergreen Forest separated them from the Swamp.

"But I like dragonflies," interrupted Becky. "The dragonflies we have back home are fun to play with," Becky began to explain.

"Once, a blue one landed on my knee and stayed there for a zillion years

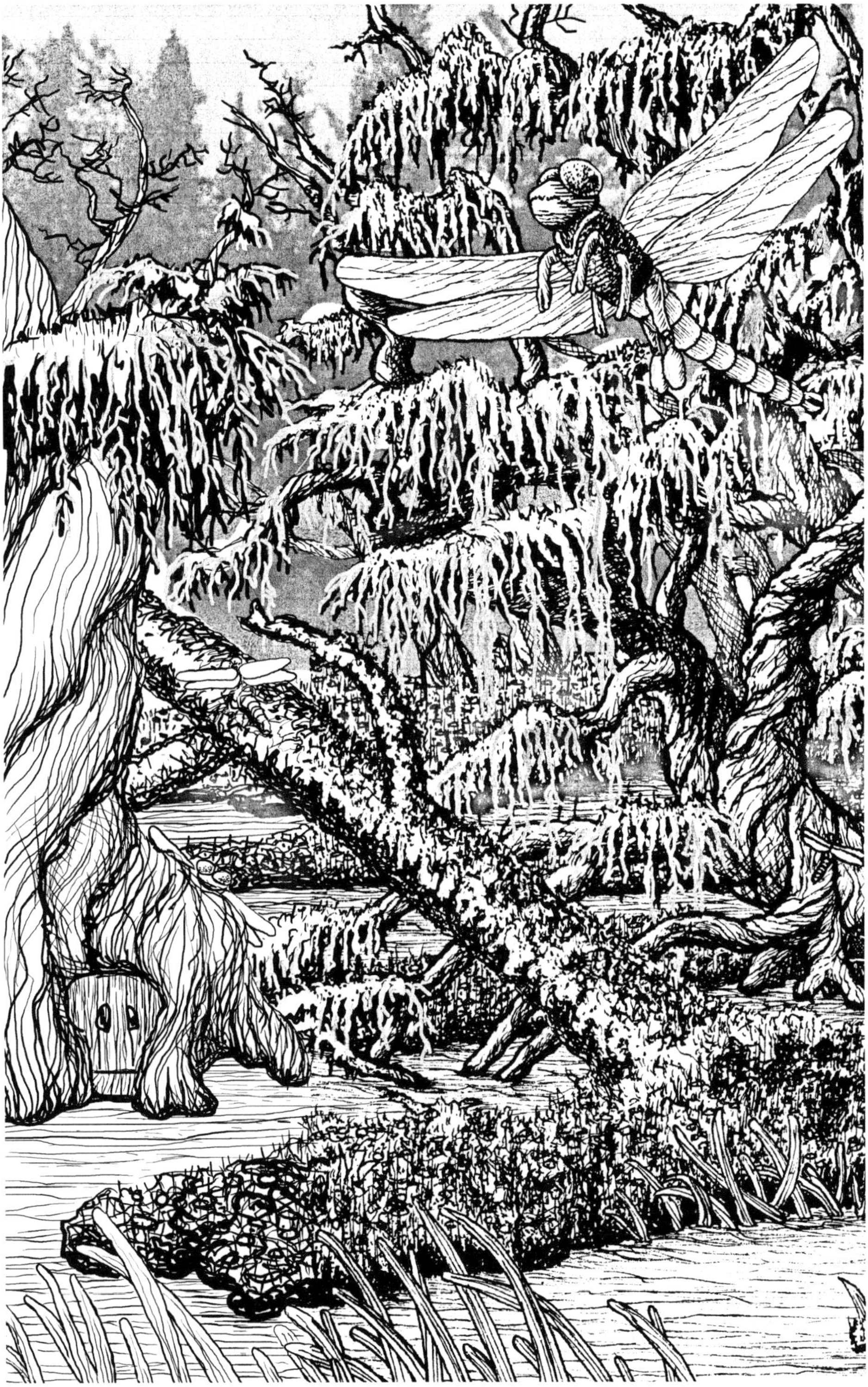

and didn't hurt me at all."

"Well, Becky, these dragonflies are a lot different than the ones you know about," explained the Princess. "Dragonflies, as you know them, are not the same as those in the Lugaluk Swamp."

"That's right, Becky. The Dragonflies here are not at all like the ones you have back home, not at all," added one of the guards.

Now that they could see that they had aroused Joey's curiosity and empathy, they wanted to continue their story.

The Lugaluks stood about the same size as the Ookees. Their clothes were not flowing and graceful, but straight and tight fitting. This kind of clothing enabled the Lugaluks to slip through openings in the roots of their tree trunk homes so they could get inside. The swamp grass was woven into materials for clothing. They also tied and braided swamp grass into nets for capturing their prey.

The high spots in the center of their swamp Village were the gathering place for the Lugaluks. Here they would take their meals and plan their war-like strategies.

Lugaluks ate nuts, gathered from the Evergreen Forest, and drank from the waters in the Swamp. Because they were so lazy, they wanted the Ookees for their slaves. They wanted them to gather their food, clean their messy Swamp, and fan them with their wings to keep them cool on days that were too hot. Unlike the Meadow Ookees, the Lugaluks had no real mission in life except to eat, sleep and cause trouble for their neighbors in and around the Valley.

Lugaluks spent their days planning ways to capture Ookees and make them slaves. Then the Ookees families would be sad and unhappy. The Dragonflies could not stand the happiness of the Ookees. Making even one of Ookees unhappy was considered a success to them.

To protect themselves against the inevitable and ongoing invasions of the Lugaluks, the Ookees kept constant guard at the border of the Evergreen Forest. The

Evergreen Forest was a lush oasis of fragrant trees, which separated their Meadow of flowers from the gloomy, frightening Lugaluk Swamp. A babbling brook passed through the Evergreen Forest and edged the Swamp on its way southward.

The Lugaluks hid among the trees of the forest, waiting for a chance to invade the Meadow to capture any weary or unsuspecting Ookees.

Captain Dredgell, an especially evil Dragonfly, was the Lugaluks leader. His brown, swamp hair coat was gathered at the waist with a soft bark belt. These same soft bark straps crossed each other on his chest and back in military fashion. The straps were studded with metal nuggets, gathered from the bed of the babbling brook. His boots were sewn from dried brown and green moss patches. They were laced with braided swamp grass.

Dredgell never stopped plotting ways to capture the Ookees. His only goal was to make all those gentle Ookees his slaves and have them do his bidding.

CHAPTER NINE
The Decision

By the time the Princess had finished with her story of the Ookees and the Lugaluks, their stomachs were growling and the sun was shining directly over head.

"Oh my, it's time for lunch," said the Princess.

"How do you know that?" asked Joey, not seeing a watch of any kind on her tiny wrist.

"Oh, that's easy," she explained. "To the Ookees, the sun rising is morning, the sun directly overhead is midday, and the sun setting is evening. Right now, the sun is directly over head. It's midday and time for lunch. Besides, my stomach is growling."

"So that's how you tell time," said

Joey, pleased with his understanding of the situation. "It's the same way that the Native Americans of our Old West told time."

"Who are Native Americans?" asked Tatashee.

Before Joey had a chance to answer, Becky interrupted him.

"I think it's midday too," said Becky, rubbing her stomach. "I'm growling too."

Joey, the guards, and the Princess Tatashee laughed.

"We are going back to our village for the midday meal now. Would you like us to come back with some food for the two of you?" Princess Tatashee asked.

Joey knew that his sister needed some good food. He was very young, but he still took his responsibility of taking care of Becky seriously.

"I guess it'll be okay," said Joey, skeptical of the incredible story told to them by the little people he had just met. He still worried about what the Ookees were going to do with them.

After the Ookees left, Joey sat and

stared into space. He was trying to absorb everything that had happened to them in the last few hours and to understand it. Could he believe all that he had heard? He wasn't completely convinced that he wasn't really dreaming the whole thing.

"What's the matter, Joey?" asked Becky.

"Nothing, I'm just thinking," He replied.

"Thinking about what?"

"About all of this! What do you think?" he snapped at her.

Becky said nothing but put her head down and let it rest in her hands. She stared at the grass below her. She could tell by the tone of her brother's voice, that she had said something to make him angry.

Joey looked over at Becky and felt bad for yelling at her. After all, she was so young. She really didn't grasp the entire situation and its problems. She only knew that she was safe and having fun with the little people. It was really better that way. If she did understand as her brother did, she might worry. It would do her no good to worry as he was.

"I'm sorry Becky. I didn't mean to snap at you like that, but don't you think that this whole thing is just a little weird?"

"No, I just think it's a wonderful a, a da, benture."

"Yes, I guess it is an adventure," Joey laughed. He grabbed her and wrestled her to the ground. They were still wrestling around on the soft green floor of the Meadow when the Ookees returned. They stopped their play immediately for fear of harming one of the Ookees.

The Ookees had carried some large pots back with them. The pots were for the two children to eat from. Although large in the Ookees hands, they seemed only to be small bowls in their large hands.

Joey and Becky started their Ookee meal. King Baldwin and Queen Rameena entered the small clearing where the children were sitting.

"How is your nectar soup?" asked the Queen.

"This is soup?" Joey was surprised. "I thought it was dessert."

All the Ookees then started to laugh.

"Then that must mean you like it, am I right?" asked Queen Rameena.

"You are definitely right," said Joey. "You know, I could get used to this very easily."

"Me too," Becky added, flecks of nectar dripping down her chin.

The nectar soup was sweet and thick, much like the fruit syrup the children were used to at home. This was a basic food for the Ookees, but a real treat for the children.

As soon as their midday meal was over, the King asked Joey to tell him a little about himself and his sister. He also asked where they had come from. Joey didn't answer right away, but looked in the direction of Becky. Queen Rameena saw immediately that Joey was a little uncomfortable talking in front of his little sister.

"Becky, how would you like to go for a walk with Princess Tatashee and look at the flowers? Maybe there is something out there that you have never seen before," said the Queen. "That is if it's all right with your brother."

Joey nodded as if to say yes. The Princess Tatashee was excited at the thought. She rushed over to where Becky was sitting.

"Bend down and place your hand in the grass so I can climb on it,

Becky," said the Princess, thrilled at the idea.

Adventure was a part of her inner soul; and this was to be a great one. In that way, she and Becky were much alike. Both loved an adventure.

Becky bent over slightly and placed her hand flat on the ground next to the Princess. Tatashee stepped up and onto her hand.

"Bring up your fingers now, Becky," the Princess said. She bent down and started to pull on Becky's fingers.

Becky did as she was asked. Now, Tatashee held tightly to Becky's curled up fingers. In this way, the Princess could now direct Becky where she wanted to go, closer to the village.

"All right Becky, you can stand up now," Queen Rameena said as she motioned to her to get up. "You must walk slowly and carefully."

"Oh I will," whispered Becky, in awe over the situation. She didn't take her eyes off the Princess; she now held in the palm of her hand.

Becky was extremely gentle. The Princess was thrilled and excited at being so high up. She could see things; she had never seen before, looking down from high over head. The best part was the safe feeling she had in the center of Becky's hand. She also knew that she could glide to the ground on her own power if need be, still having her wings.

As Becky walked, she was careful to make sure that her movements were smooth. She did not want anything to happen to Princess Tatashee.

It was strange for Joey to see his younger

sister taking such good care of someone else for a change. He always had to take care of Becky and look out for her. Since she was the youngest, she hadn't had anyone to take care of.

Soon they were on their way. They headed toward the Ookee Village.

"Now that Becky is gone, do you think you can tell us, in greater detail, what circumstances brought you to us?" asked the Queen tenderly, breaking into Joey's thoughts.

Joey sat back, feeling a little more comfortable with the Ookees. He began to explain what had happened to Becky and him.

He told the Ookees they moved to a new home after their father got his new job. He explained the ride to school, and that the lightning had hit the covered bridge. He explained how afraid he was for his sister and himself when they fell into the raging waters. He hadn't dared to say that in front of Becky. He told the Ookees about their watery ride down the stream in the rain. Then he told the Ookees about their adventures coming to the Meadow where they were now.

The King and Queen sat and talked with Joey for a long time. He felt more secure when they said they would work as hard as they could to find a way to return them to their home. Finally Bennet, the trusted royal tender, came and stood by the royal couple.

"Joey, this is Bennet, our friend. He has been with us for as long as I can remember. He lives with us in the castle and tends to our every need. He is like one of our own family," announced King Baldwin.

"How do you do," Joey bowed from his sitting position.

"Oh, heck, darn don't bow to me," Bennet said embarrassed. "Just kick back and say 'Hi ya there'."

"All right. Hi ya there," Joey said as they all laughed.

"We were getting a bit worried. I decided to come and check on the three of you," explained Bennet.

"Why in the world would you be worried about us?" asked the King, a little put out. "We had the guards and Joey here."

The King never looked towards Joey when he said this. He knew he had made Joey feel good to think that the King, all powerful, felt safe because he was around. He was right, for Joey's face brightened at hearing what the King had said.

"Because, your highness, it is time for dinner. It is getting cold," Bennet responded. "I have never known you to miss a meal before."

"My, my, is it that late already?" said the Queen, as she stood and brushed off her dress.

King Baldwin looked up towards the sky. "By gosh, it sure is getting late. Where does the time go?"

"We put Becky at the base of the Great Northern Mountains to rest and have her dinner. Shall I take Joey there as well?" asked Bennet. "That way they can be closer together and closer to the village as well. No Ookee goes there after the evening meal. The two of them can stand up, stretch their legs, and walk around the mountain paths."

"Yes, Bennet, please do," said the Queen.

"Oh, and Bennet, have some of the others make them some sort of softness to sleep on; also give them something to keep them warm tonight."

"All ready taken care of, Your Highness," he answered.

Bennet took Joey to a place to wash up, and from there to where Becky was already having her dinner.

"Oh, Baldwin, the poor children. You must let them stay," the Queen said compassionately, as the two of them walked back towards the village.

"Of course, Rameena, I said they could stay; but their parents must be terribly worried, about out of their minds by now. You heard how Joey spoke of them. They are very loving and giving. They have to be sick with worry.

"Somehow, we must find a way to get the children home. Unfortunately, we can't send them home the way they came. We will have to find another way."

CHAPTER TEN
Anthony Joins the Search

The people of the town where Joey and Becky lived with their parents were terribly worried. The town's people and the sheriff's department had been searching for the children the entire day.

They had very few clues to Joey and Becky's whereabouts. The children seemed to have disappeared into thin air.

The sheriff was at the children's home now. He was talking to Joey and Becky's parents, the Mitchell's, about the efforts of the entire town to find their children.

The sun was going down, and the search had been called off until the next morning. There was no sense of keeping up the search in the dark. The Sheriff was afraid that if they searched in the dark they might miss a clue to where the children had disappeared.

"We have looked everywhere in the vicinity of the stream and cannot find the children anywhere. The only thing we know for sure is that the children fell into the stream."

"As you know, we found the bikes on the bridge. The bikes were next to the hole that the lightning caused when it hit. One of my deputies found this small piece of cloth hanging on one of the branches that edged the stream. Your friend said it was from Becky's shirt. Unfortunately, that is all they found. As I said, there was no sign of the children anywhere."

Mrs. Mitchell, Peggy, grabbed for the small swatch of material that the sheriff was holding.

"Where did you find this?" asked Mrs. Mitchell as she held the swatch of cloth that had been a part of her little girl's clothing.

"About five miles south of where the children fell in. We found it in a very remote area. It was hanging on a branch that drooped out over the stream," began the sheriff. "The ground is covered with moss, and the trees there are very thick. We could find no footprints. There is a path that leads to the woods. The path seems to disappear just inside the heavy growth there. We checked every nook and cranny there. We didn't want to leave any stone unturned. Unfortunately, we didn't find a thing."

"Then this means that they are still alive," Peggy Mitchell said, hugging the piece of cloth and weeping for joy.

"That's right," her husband, Jonathan Mitchell, said. He held his wife and wept with her.

"We're going to leave you now," said the sheriff. "We will be starting the search again at first light in the morning.

"Thank you. Thank you and the rest of the town," said Peggy and Jonathan Mitchell in unison, shaking the sheriff's hand and trying to wipe the tears from their faces.

"Okay everyone, go home now," said the sheriff. "We will be starting again bright and early in the morning. All of you must get some sleep. You'll need all the strength you can muster for the search tomorrow."

The crowd, one by one, started to disperse. Soon the Mitchell's front yard was empty.

"This is rough," said the Sheriff to one of his deputies. "It has been one whole day, and nothing but a piece of cloth has been turned up. I wired the towns downstream to watch out for the children. So far, no one has seen anything of Joey or Becky.

"All we have to go by is that small piece of cloth. It could mean that only Becky has managed to make it to the shore of the river stream. Another possibility is that Becky's shirt was caught on the branch as the children tried to get out of the water. Maybe then they and were swept away with the current. Neither may have escaped the water, it was so furious during the storm."

"No, that's not true," shouted Peggy. "They did get out of the water. I know they did," she said, standing in their doorway and listening to what was just said. "And you can bet your life that if one has gotten to safety, that the other one is with them," she cried, almost hysterical.

"Of course, we were just..." the Sheriff stopped and motioned for his deputies to leave with him. What had been said could not be taken back. He wanted to just put an end to it there. As they left, the Mitchell's stood on the porch in each other's arms.

Soon after the sheriff and his deputies left the Mitchell's house, it began to grow darker. The night and its darkness had completely settled in.

Next door, an elderly gentleman sat on his porch, rocking in the cool evening air. He had been known to sit there for an entire day without going inside and, without saying anything. He never spoke much to anyone. The town considered him quite odd. He had overheard the conversation that the sheriff was having with the Mitchell's. He had begun to smile.

Soon after the sheriff and his deputies had left the Mitchell's, it began to grow darker. The night and its darkness had completely settled in.

"The children will be just fine. Don't y'all be frettin' anymore," the voice of the old man next door interrupted. "The little people will take good care of them kiddies. You wait an' see."

Mrs. Mitchell looked across the yard in the direction of the old man's house. "What little people?" Peggy asked with real concern in her voice. "Do you know something about my children?"

"Only that they will be fine."

"How do you know that?" she asked.

"Don't pay attention to him," her husband interrupted. "You know that everyone says he's very eccentric."

"No, I want to hear more," she said as she got up and walked across the yard. The old man was slowly rocking back and forth in his chair.

"What are you talking about?" she asked again.

"I'm talking about the little people. The children will be safe enough with them; I know."

"Come on, dear. You're just listening to the ravings of a crazy old man," her husband urged. He was angry at the thought that the old man, who had sat on the porch next door from them daily since they moved in, would choose this time to decide to speak to them in such gibberish.

"Don't let him bother you. Tomorrow, the search party is going to concentrate on the area further downstream to see if the children had been around there."

"But what if they don't find them down stream?" she asked with tears still in her eyes.

"Then, I'll start searching myself, in the place where they found the piece of Becky's shirt. One way or the other, we'll find them," her husband promised.

As the Mitchell's walked away from their neighbor's porch, the old man began to feel sorry for them. He knew that the children were not in the direction they were about to search the next day and their parents would be worried even more when their efforts turned up nothing. He also knew that if Mr. Mitchell made good on his promise to his wife, he would eventually come upon the Valley known to him as a small boy. He decided to do something about it himself.

CHAPTER ELEVEN
Attack on the Meadow

Meanwhile, back in the Swamp of Fantasy Valley, Captain Dredgell was on the warpath again, or we should say, still on the warpath. Dredgell had gathered his eager soldiers to the highest spot in the swamp.

At his side were his sons, Bracks and Deeker. Bracks was his older son. He was just like his father. He loved the planning and fighting of wars.

On the other hand, Deeker was just the opposite. His strategies always included a plan for peace. He was ashamed of the evil ways of his father and brother and the Lugaluks that followed them.

He couldn't understand why they hated the Ookees. He tried to change them into good, peaceful creatures with a noble purpose to life, but the other Lugaluks just laughed at him.

"We are warriors and not an Ookee-loving sissy like you," rang out their cries of outrage; led of course, by his brother, Bracks.

Deeker was constantly laughed at and put down for his way of thinking. He knew that most of the Lugaluks were not like his father and brother, but they were too scared to say anything. Most of the Lugaluks, he felt, would much rather be using their time on more useful things rather than always planning wars and starting trouble.

Their fear of the Captain was greater than their personal wants in life. So they followed every rule, every command of their leaders, no matter how wrong they felt they were. They never showed that they disagreed with those commands, or that they agreed at all with Deeker's peace loving ways.

Tonight, a full moon was expected. It

would be the perfect night to attack the Meadow. There would be just enough light to see the unsuspecting Ookees. Capturing them should not pose too much of a problem, they hoped.

"My mighty Lugaluks," Captain Dredgell roared from the high spot where his soldiers had gathered. Standing straight and tall, with his dragonfly wings spread wide in war-like fashion, he shouted to his crowd of loyal followers.

"Tonight, you will arm yourselves with swamp grass nets. Then you will attack Ookee Meadow and capture many slaves."

The soldiers shouted their approval and flapped their wings in thunderous applause.

Then Bracks stood before them. The Lugaluk Soldiers fell silent as they waited for him to speak.

"Tonight, we will bring great honor to the Lugaluk Army," Bracks shouted.

The soldiers roared in agreement. Bracks raised his hands to silence them.

The Ookees ~ Page 112

Then he turned to Captain Dredgell.

"Father, not only will we bring you many Ookee slaves to do your bidding," he said with his eyes flashing bright orange with anticipation,"but we will also bring you the greatest prize of all. Our gift to you will be to deliver to you the Princess. Tonight we will either deliver to you the Princess Tatashee, or return in disgrace."

Once again, the soldiers raised their voices in a shout of excitement that shook the trees.

Dredgell gave them an evil smile. His eyes were opened wide with excitement at the thought of finally realizing his goal of capturing the royal Princess. He would keep her a hostage, a prisoner, a powerful tool in his trading amongst his own enemies.

Dredgell put his hands up, the evil grin still lurking on his face.

"If you bring the Princess to me, there will be rewards beyond your wildest dreams," announced the Captain.

Again, his soldiers shouted his praises. They roared with great excitement.

The Captain silenced them again. His eyes shown fire red as he said, "But if you fail to capture the Ookee Princess this time, I'll have all your wings clipped. You will be banished to the Muckland until your wings grow back. That will take a very long, long time."

The soldiers were silent. Only the sound of their trembling knees knocking together could be heard. They weren't so sure they wanted such a challenge now for they knew the Captain meant what he had threatened. He would make good his words if they failed.

Before they had time to think about it, orders rang out from the Captain.

"Away with you!" Captain Dredgell commanded. "Away with you all to the Ookee's Meadow. Fly straight and strong to your destination."

The sounds of their wings buzzed loudly in the stillness of the night. In formation, the soldiers flew boldly through the trees of the Evergreen Forest that edged their dark and murky Swamp. They flew straight towards the Ookee Meadow.

Most of the Ookees, unaware of the danger that threatened them, were fast asleep in their tulip homes. The Ookees had made Becky and Joey a bed under the branches of the maple trees at the base of the Great Northern Mountains. There, they had fallen sound asleep. Only a handful of guards were standing watch at the edge of the Meadow, since everything in Ookee Valley had been so calm and quiet for quite some time.

"What's that sound?" said Skimp, King Baldwin's bravest and most trusted guard.

"I don't hear anything," answered Pleeter.

But Skimp was sure he had heard something. Pleeter was young and still quite unreliable because of his lack of experience. Although, everyone felt he would one day be a capable guard, he now spent too much time day dreaming about the young Ookee maidens. These

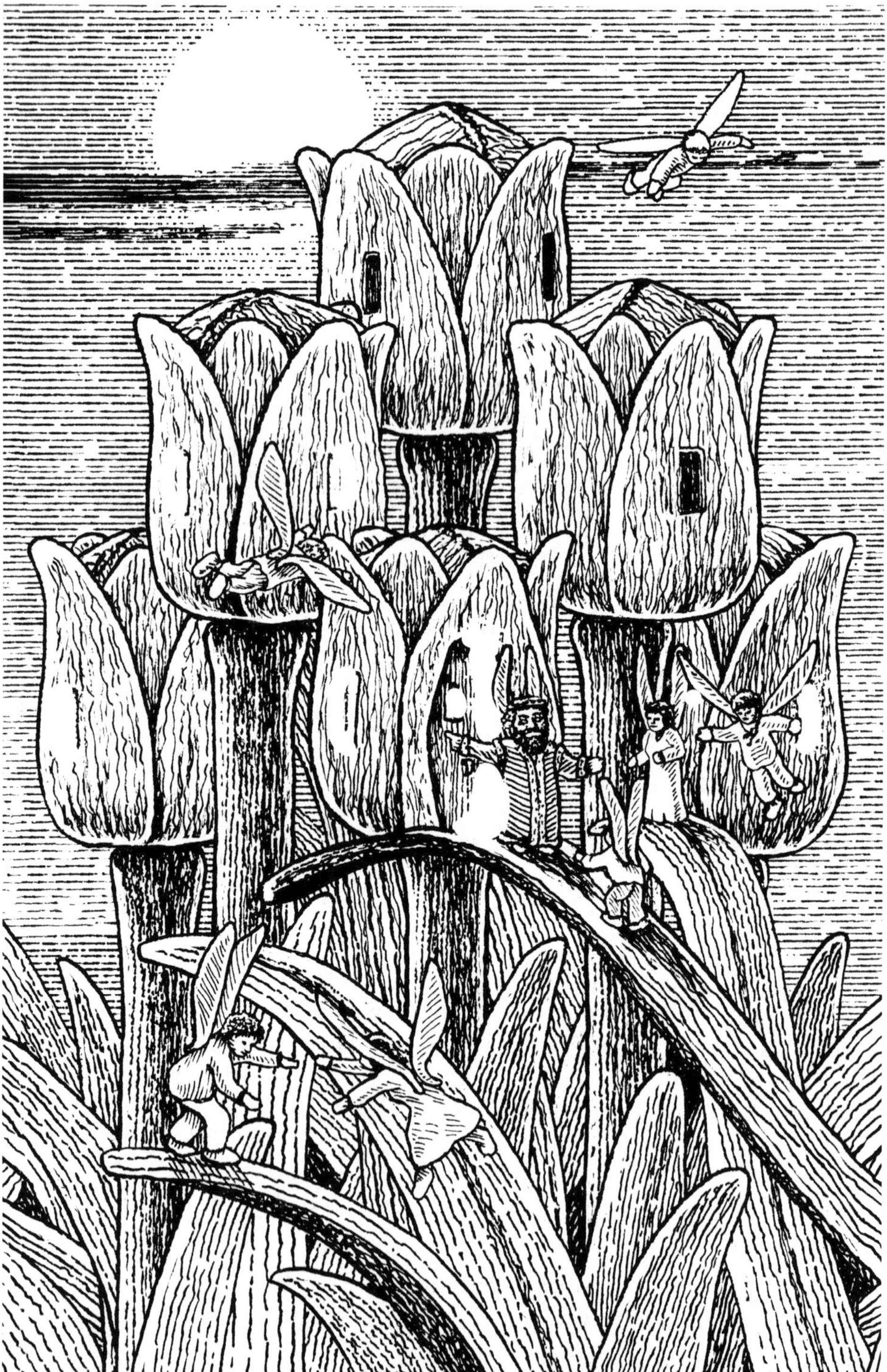

days, you couldn't trust Pleeter to hear a bomb going off right next to him. Even with his faults, he was still a good guard, one that could be trusted in the face of danger. Next to Skimp, he was one of the bravest guards watching over the Meadow.

Skimp strained his ears. Yes, there it was, he heard it again. Only now, he knew what the sound was. The wind was carrying the sounds through the trees of the Evergreen Forest. It was the beating of wings, many, many wings. Only the brazen and treacherous Lugaluks would fly at night.

"Pleeter!" Skimp yelled. "Sound the alarm. The Lugaluks are coming. We must send out the warning."

Pleeter and the other guards grabbed their lily horns and blew them fiercely and loudly as they could.

Awooo! Awooo! Awooo! Awooo! Awooo! Awooo! Awooo rang out the sounds from the boundaries of the Evergreen Forest.

As the blaring horns echoed throughout the Meadow, the sleeping Ookees were aroused from their beds. They quickly flew to the white tulip castle where King Baldwin was waiting for them.

The frightened Ookees trembled with fear, as they cried to their King, "King Baldwin, what is wrong?"

"Why has a warning been sounded?"

"What's happening?"

"Are we in danger?" The Ookees shouted out, one after the other.

"I don't know," Baldwin told them, "but there is some kind of trouble brewing. Hurry to the far edge of the Meadow and hide in the blossoms of the Lilac Bush. Take Queen Rameena and the Princess with you. Protect them and yourselves at all costs. Off with you now, and quickly," the King said, avoiding anymore questions.

They needed to hurry, if the Ookees were to get to safety before trouble hit, what ever it was. A mad rush of Ookees could be seen, flying towards the Babbling Brook where the Majestic Lilac Bush stood. It was tall and powerful in size. It looked as if was calling the Ookees to safety hide among its strong and thick branches.

As the last Ookee was seen entering the protection of the Lilac Bush, King Baldwin flew to the guard post. He came to rest next to Skimp.

"What is it, Skimp?" the King asked, having a feeling he already knew the answer.

"It's the Lugaluks, Sire," Skimp told him.

"They are coming through the Evergreen Forest, I fear, to attack us,"

"I was afraid it was that," Baldwin said, "but we are ready for them this time. The Lugaluks will have a little surprise coming."

Suddenly, hoards of tiny blinking lights filled the sky over the meadow. They were coming from the meadow west of the Babbling Brook. They moved quickly towards King Baldwin, Skimp, and the fast approaching Lugaluks.

"It's the Fireflies!" Pleeter yelled. "They are coming to help us battle the Lugaluks."

The Fireflies made their home in the Fertile Valley beyond the Fragrant Lilac Bush. They despised the evil ways of the Lugaluks. They would do everything in their power to send them back to their damp and murky Swamp before they could take away or do any harm to any of the inhabitants of Ookee Valley.

King Brightness, their leader, had promised Baldwin that he would send his soldiers whenever he heard the alarm. King Brightness had kept his promise.

At the base of the Great Northern Mountain where the children from the outside world were sleeping, Becky started to stir. She began rubbing her eyes. The lights from the Fireflies, swarming in the sky above, were so bright that they had disturbed her sleep. She sighed as she yawned. Her eyes started to blink and open. As they opened completely, the lights over head amazed her.

"Joey! Joey!" She called to her brother in her excitement, but Joey didn't stir. He was deep in a sound sleep.

"Joey! Joey!" She shouted again. This time she reached over and shook Joey, as she called out his name.

"Joey! Joey! Look!" She called persistently.

"What Becky, what do you want? What's wrong?" He said as he tried to come to his senses.

"Nothings wrong, only look," she said as she pointed over head.

"Wow!" seemed to be all that Joey could say in reply to her. "Look at all those lights."

"Wa da ya spose it is?" asked Becky, straining her neck to look up.

"Some kind of a celebration, I guess," Joey answered, still focusing his attention on the sights above the Meadow. "Remember that everything here is different from home. It could be something that happens every night."

How could they know that the lights

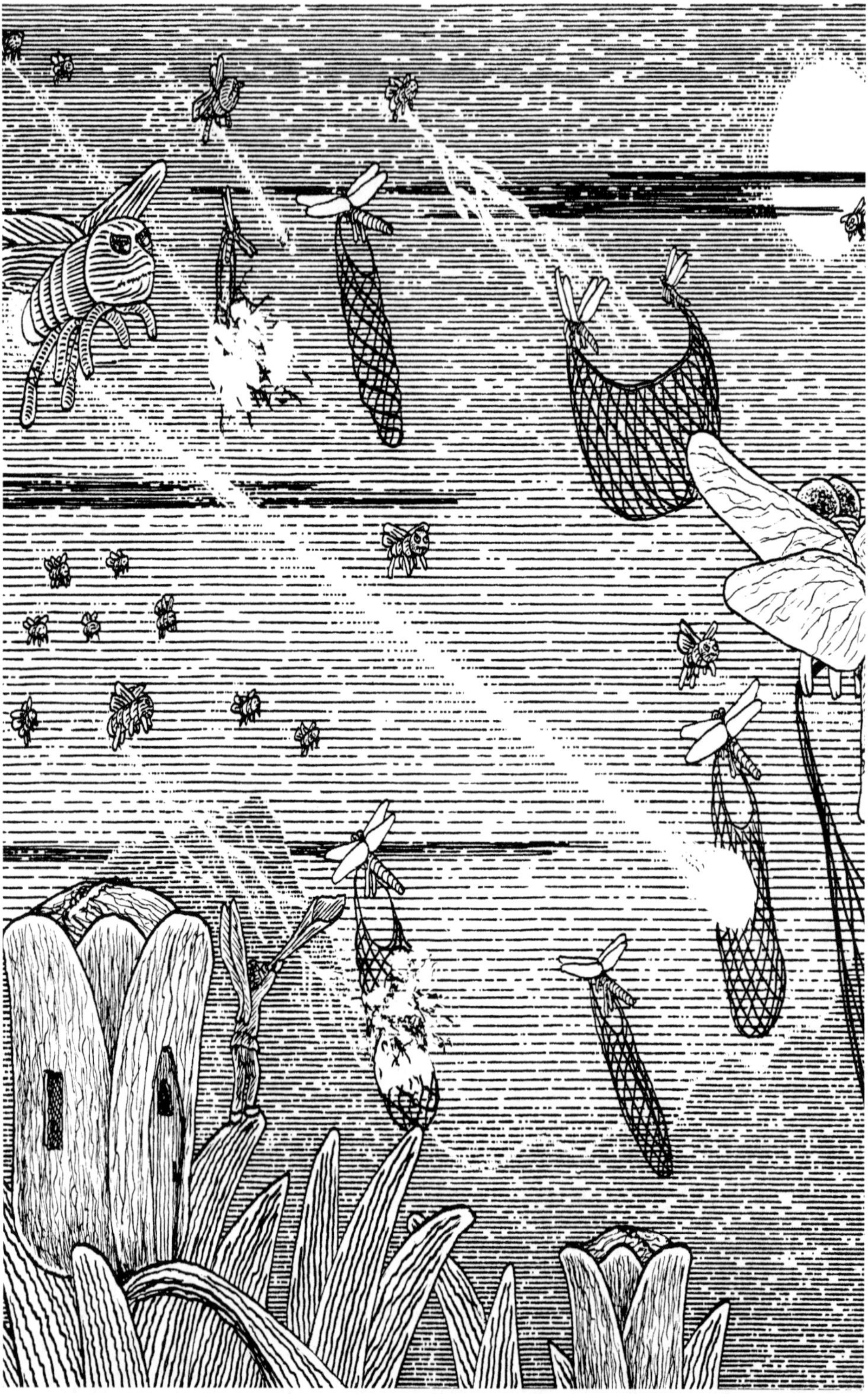

over head were for no celebration?

The sounds of the Lugaluks coming could be heard much more clearly now. They must be almost to the boundary of the Evergreen Forest. Everyone was ready and awaiting their uninvited entrance into the Ookee Meadow.

The Lugaluks, led by Bracks, burst confidently from the Evergreen Forest. Their wings were flapping wildly as they flew closer to the Meadow where the Ookees were. Their swamp grass nets were spread wide; ready to swoop over any poor, unfortunate Ookee they came across.

As soon as the Lugaluks appeared, the Fireflies began throwing bolts of lightning and balls of fire at the Lugaluks' nets. As lightning and fire hit them, the nets burst into flames. Every time the Lugaluk Soldiers would throw one of their nets down to trap an Ookee; one of the Fireflies would throw a lightning bolt or fireball and destroy the net in mid air.

"Look out Skimp!" shouted Pleeter. "Behind you."

Skimp ducked just in time as one of

the nets just missed him.

Whhhiiissshhh! WHAP! SSSSSSSSSS the sounds were heard. A fireball shot across the sky and hit the Lugaluk net. It burst into flames before it could hit the ground.

"To your right, King Brightness," shouted Skimp, as a net was fast approaching him.

Whirrr, Whirrr, Whirrr, came the sound of it twirling through the air in the Firefly's King's direction. He dipped in the air, just escaping its threatening web.

Whhhiiissshhh came the sound of a fireball, whizzing past Skimp's head and landing on the ominous net that had just missed the King of the Fireflies. *WHAP! SSSSSSSSSS,* another net burned to ashes.

"Brightness!" yelled King Baldwin. "Some of the Lugaluks have eluded our lines of defense and are heading in the direction of the Lilac Bush."

"Not to worry," King Brightness said as he ducked. Another net had just missed him. "It's time for stage two, I expect. Look!"

As he pointed in the direction of the

The Ookies ~ Page 74

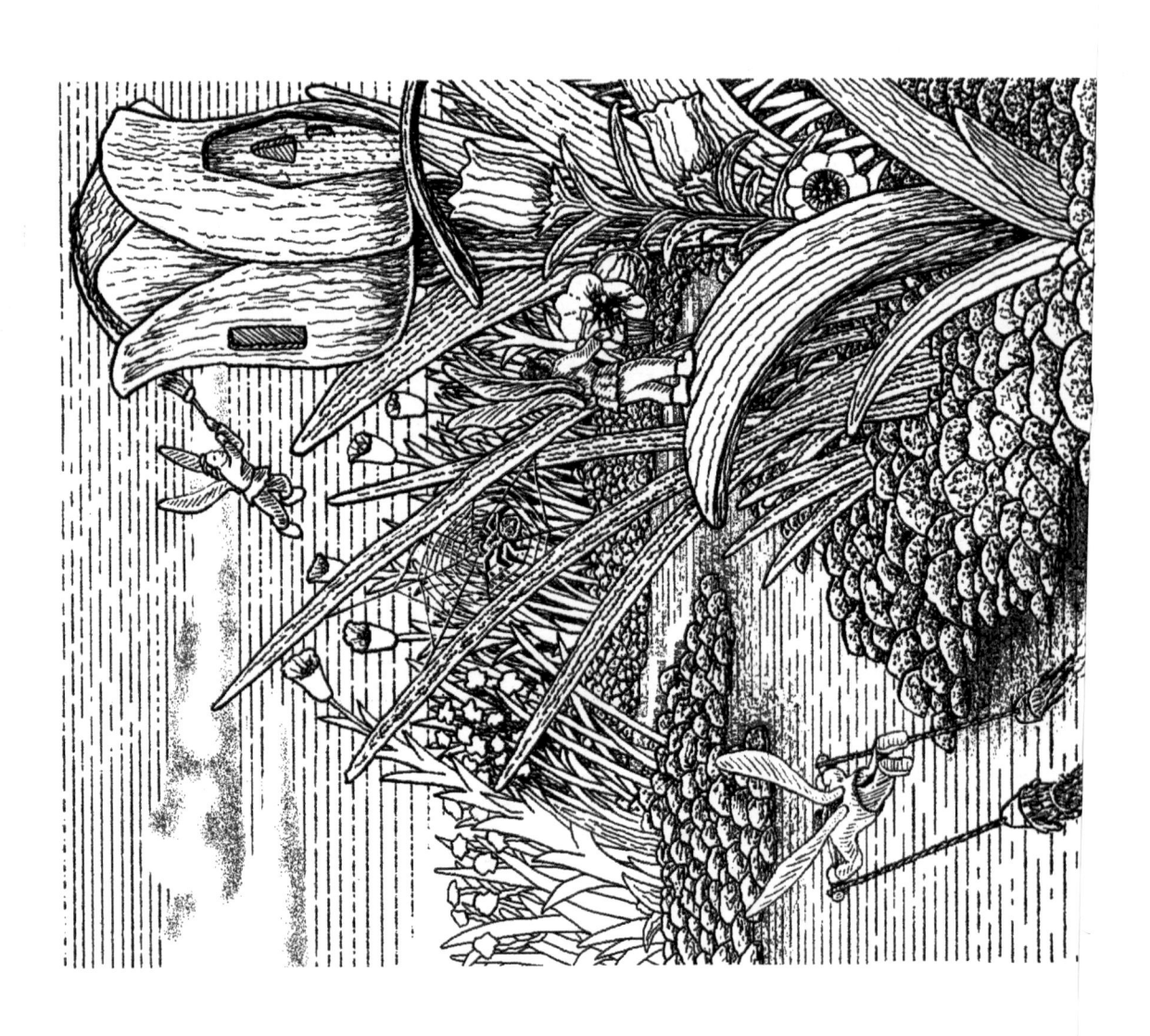

threatening Dragonflies, who were just about to find, unexpectedly, the women of the village in the Lilac Bushes, another round of Fireflies rose from the ground below and started their attack.

WHAP, SSSS, WHAP, SSSS, WHAP, SSSS, WHAP, SSSS were the sounds coming from fireballs. They hit the nets of the Lugaluk force that had eluded them. Flames shot up everywhere in the skies over head. The Lugaluk nets were hit and burned before the intruding army knew what was happening.

The frenzy of fireballs, swamp grass nets and bolts of lightning went on for some time. The moonlit sky over the Meadow was made much brighter by the lightning and fire show.

The whirling of the nets being thrown, the sounds of the fireballs or lightning bolts, the *WHAP* when the two came together, and the sounds of the nets burning eliminated any threat of a capture.

"I should be out there, fighting those miserable Dragonflies," shouted Bennet.

He shook a stick at the sky where all the fighting was going on. "I would knock their blocks off," he said as he lost his balance and toppled onto the ground.

"Are you okay?" asked the Princess as he started to get up.

"I'm okay. It's just my pride that's hurt, that's all," Bennet answered, as he flew up to the branch where she was sitting with her mother.

"Why, Bennet, how could your pride be hurt?" asked the Queen.

"How do you think? I'm the only man here. I should be out there, fighting shoulder to shoulder with the rest of the men."

"Bennet, if you were out there, who would be here protecting all of us?" asked the Queen, trying to build up his ego. "What if one of those nets got past the Fireflies? Or worse yet, one of the Lugaluks were to get by them and get to us? If you were not here, who would be here to protect us?"

"I never really thought of it that way," he replied. He was still unsatisfied not being in on the fighting.

"That's right, Bennet," added the Princess. "Father trusts you to stand watch over all of us, and that's why you are here. We feel quite safe with you here to protect us, Bennet. Father once said that if he couldn't be with us for any reason; we would be all right as long as we were with you."

Bennet's ego was back in place. It was a little larger than normal now. He was feeling much better.

Soon, the fighting was all over. The Fireflies had burned all of the Lugaluks nets and destroyed any means of capturing the Ookees. Bracks was furious. The Lugaluk nets were all destroyed.

The force and furry of the protecting Fireflies was so intense that it sent the attacking Dragonflies scurrying for their lives. One by one, the Lugaluk soldiers turned and flew back to the safety of the swamp. They left empty-handed. They had no captives, and all of their nets were burned. Their tails were curled up behind them in fear of being caught themselves. They headed for the security of the high branches of the Evergreen Forest and to the safety of Lugaluk Swamp that lies on the other side.

As he reluctantly followed his retreating army, Bracks yelled back to the Ookees and the Fireflies. "You have not heard the last from us. Captain Dredgell will make you all pay for what you have done," he said, as he shook his fist at the meadow. He then vanished into the trees of the Evergreen Forest.

CHAPTER TWELVE
The Celebration

"Hurray!" yelled Skimp, Pleeter, and the rest of the guards.

"Hurray for the Fireflies! Together we have sent the Lugaluks scurrying like swamp rats. Three cheers for our friends. Hip, hip, hurray! Hip, hip, hurray! Hip, hip, hurray!"

The Fireflies could be seen, coming down to where the Ookees had already assembled. Shouts of joy and excitement could be heard everywhere. A few stayed in the skies over head to stand guard. They wanted to make sure that none of the Lugaluks would change their minds and return to capture any unsuspecting Ookee or Firefly for that matter.

"Yes," King Baldwin said. "Our friends, the Fireflies, have saved us from the

The Ookees ~ Page 130

wicked Lugaluks. This calls for a celebration."

"First, someone must go and let the others know that we are all fine. They can go back to their homes."

The young guard, Pleeter, was sent to tell the Ookees that everyone was okay. No one had been hurt. It was safe to leave the sheltering blossoms of the Lilac Bush and return to their homes in the village.

The Fireflies stood talking to the Ookee Guards for a few minutes more before returning to their homes as well. They left the Ookee Guards to keep watch.

Before they parted, the Fireflies and King Brightness were invited, as guests of honor, to a party to be given by the Ookees the next night. The very best nectar would be set out for the occasion. The freshest cool spring water from the stream would be drawn to toast the brave and loyal Fireflies.

Everyone did his or her share to clean

up the meadow from the battle of the night before. It was strange to be picking up so much swamp grass from inside their borders. The ashes from the burning nets had to be swept off the roofs of some of their tulip homes.

The Ookees loved doing the work that needed to be done in preparing for a celebration. Soon, they were finished. Everything was clean and neat again. There were no signs left of the war with the beings of the Swamp.

Becky and Joey sat and played at the base of the Great Northern Mountains, while the Ookees were busy cleaning. They didn't dare enter the Meadow with all the Ookees busy at work. It would put the little people at risk if they did.

The Ookees finished their work none too soon. Their honored guests, the Fireflies, were seen in the distance, heading for the Village. As the Fireflies arrived, the Ookees cheered and motioned for them to take their places at the tables.

"Thank you, dear friends," King

Baldwin said, as he raised his cup to honor those who had saved them from disaster. "Dredgell and the Lugaluks may be our enemies, but we are fortunate and grateful to have many more friends than foes." Loud clapping and raised voices cheered in agreement.

"I propose a toast, a toast to our friends and allies, the Fireflies."

"Here, Here!" came the roar of approval from the Ookees. They raised their glasses in honor to their guests, and drank in unison.

"And now, let the celebration begin," announced King Baldwin, as he took the chair next to King Brightness.

Everyone ate and drank their fill. It was the beginning of a festive night of fun with their friends.

King Baldwin knew that Captain Dredgell, as well as Bracks had threatened to return with a vengeance; but he was no longer as worried as he had been. They were not alone in their battle against the Lugaluks anymore. Besides, this was a party. Only happy thoughts should be in their heads now.

Before the party was fully under way, King Baldwin told King Brightness about Becky and Joey and gave a brief explanation of why they were there. King Baldwin and Queen Rameena took King Brightness to the base of the Great Northern Mountains. They introduced Becky and Joey, their new friends from the Outside World, to him.

"I hope you were not too frightened by the attack last night, Becky," said Brightness, hovering at shoulder height to her.

"No, Your Highness," she said, as she bowed to the King. "Joey said we were on an a ah a benchur. It sure was a doozie. I thought it was a celebration."

Everyone laughed at what Becky had said except for King Baldwin. He knew that this was a time for happiness and celebration. He also knew that Captain Dredgell would make good his promise. He would be back again. The next time, he would be better prepared. His thoughts were suddenly interrupted by the sound of his name being called in the evening air.

CHAPTER THIRTEEN
A Friend from the Past

"Prince Baldwin, are you there?" came the tremulous voice. "It's Anthony, from the past."

There was silence. Anthony could hear no answer.

"Prince Baldwin, can you hear me? Is anyone there? Can anyone hear me?"

Again, there was nothing but silence. Anthony knew he was in the right place, for he was standing in front of the thicket that had made him sleepy when he was younger. This was the thicket that separated the Ookee Meadow from the Outside World.

"Prince Baldwin, think back. Think back, and try to remember when you were a young lad. Think back to one night, when an outsider came to the meadow, frightened, wet and hungry. Do you remember? I was that outsider. Your father took me in. Try to remember, Prince Baldwin. Are you there? Are you listening to me?"

The Ookees and the Fireflies remained silent as the strange voice came rumbling over the Meadow from the direction of the thicket.

"I seem to remember something about an outsider who entered the Meadow long, long ago. It was back when I was a young lad," spoke King Brightness softly.

"Yes, there was a boy," King Baldwin whispered to King Brightness. "How could I have forgotten? But it was so long ago."

King Baldwin motioned for the Ookees to be still and to stay where they were. He and King Brightness flew in the direction of the thicket. They flew low and kept quiet as they neared the outer boundaries of their meadow.

"I see a bright light. Is that you King

Glimmer?" shouted Anthony relieved that someone was there.

"Oh, that's nice," said King Brightness in a sarcastic manner, staring down at his body. "Why didn't I just send out a beam to show we were coming?"

King Baldwin just laughed. It was sort of funny.

"No, that was my father," King Brightness answered. "I'm Brightness, his son. Remember me?"

"Yes, yes, I do," answered Anthony, even more excited.

"Is that you, Anthony," King Baldwin called out, as he flew up to greet his long lost friend.

"Yes, it is Anthony. Is that you, Prince Baldwin?"

Anthony tried to focus on the tiny being that was hovering on the other side of the thicket. He was having trouble seeing him.

"No, it's King Baldwin now," he replied with a chuckle. "What has brought you here after all this time?"

There, standing in front of them was a tall and aging man. The years had changed him, but his voice still sounded familiar. He stood there, towering over the thicket that separated the meadow from the Outside World. His face had become strained and wrinkled; yet upon closer inspection, the boyish smile and dancing eyes that King Baldwin remembered, seemed to show through. He stood hunched over a little and looked weak. It was Anthony, no doubt about it.

"I am looking for two children, a boy and a girl. They have been lost from their parents for some time now. Have you seen them?"

"So that's why you have come here after all these years. You know the children, and remembered your own experiences with us so very long ago," replied King Baldwin. "They are here, safe and well."

"Well then, that is good news," Anthony said, smiling.

He was afraid that they wouldn't be

there. He had worried about making the long trek to the Valley and interrupting the peace of the Ookee's Village for nothing. He was more afraid that if the children were not there, they might have succumbed to the raging waters of the storm filled stream. He was both happy and relieved to find that they were in the meadow and, as King Baldwin said, safe and sound.

"I have come to take them home. I was afraid the secret of your valley would be discovered if I didn't."

"Then are they beginning the search for the children in this direction?" asked King Baldwin.

"No, not yet, but it is just a matter of time before they do. Worse yet, they may stop searching. If that happens, their parents will have sadness and fear. I can prevent that, if I get the children home and soon.

"It is getting late, Anthony. Maybe you should stay and start out in the morning when you are fresh," King Baldwin said.

"No, Prince, er I mean, King Baldwin. The search will continue in the morning. I want to have the children back to the stream before the town people get there.

It was along way to get here, and I got lost a few times. It will be a long way to travel going back, but now I know the shortest route to take.

We must get started right away. We need to reach a safe distance away from here, so we won't give away the secret of this Valley. I don't want them to see the direction we come from, when we are found."

King Baldwin knew that the old man was right. The children had to go with Anthony now. The safety of the Valley and all the Ookees in it was at stake, and the children's parents must be sick with worry and half out of their minds.

As much as he would have liked to visit with an old friend, Anthony was right. They must leave right away.

By now, Skimp was standing close to where the men were talking. King Baldwin sent him to get the children.

The two kings and their friend from the past, Anthony, talked for a while. They got a little caught up on things. They discussed the fact that Baldwin and Brightness were now the ruling monarchs of their lands. Their parents had grown very old and tired and had passed away many years before.

It was good to chat about the past even though they had such a short time in which to talk. Every one knew it was important to get the children home quickly before the secret of the Ookee Meadow was discovered. Everyone knew that Anthony was right.

Skimp left word in the Meadow that everything was all right and that the children would be going home. They were told about Anthony, who had come to get the children.

Meanwhile, back at the base of the Great Northern Mountains, Becky and Joey were preparing to leave. It would be hard to say good bye, but Becky and

Joey knew they had to hurry.

Becky gathered up Pookie Bear. The two children headed off in the direction of the thicket. King Baldwin, Queen Rameena and the Princess Tatashee were waiting for them.

"Goodbye everyone. Thank you for everything," said Joey, as he stood before the two Kings.

"Good bye, Joey," replied the King Baldwin. "You and Becky must get going now. Hurry."

With Becky leading the way, the two children began to crawl through the opening that had brought them into the meadow. The angel dust did not affect them as it did when they entered, for they were leaving. The dust only caused a sleeping effect when an Outsider was entering the Valley.

Becky was the first to reach the other side. As soon as she got to her feet, she recognized the man who stood waiting for her and her brother.

"I remember you," said Becky. "You

are the nice old man who sits on the porch next door and rocks all day. You must be Anthony."

"That's right Becky. Now we are going home."

Becky was sad at the thought of leaving her friends of the Valley. Tears started to form in her eyes. She turned and waved to the Ookees, as they hovered over the branches on the other side of the thicket.

"Bye everyone," she said, as she started to cry.

"Good bye, Becky. We'll miss you," their voices rang out as they answered.

As Joey put his arm around his sister, he waved to the Ookees he had known for such a short time. He choked up as he said his good byes.

"Um, bye for now," was all he could manage to get out.

As everyone waved goodbye, the children started on their trip home with their new friend Anthony.

CHAPTER FOURTEEN
The Homecoming

"Hey, Anthony, how did you know where to find us; and how did you know the Ookees by name?" Joey asked.

"Slow down, slow down, boy. One question at a time is about all I can answer. I'm an old man, remember?" Anthony said, with a twinge of laughter in his voice as the three trudged along.

"I knew because I had been here before. That's how."

"You been here before, Anthony?" asked Becky.

"Yep, that's what I said, isn't it?"

The two of them nodded, as they kept in step with the old man. Even though Anthony walked with a cane, the children had to take some double steps in order to keep up.

While they walked, Anthony explained that he too, as a boy, got lost in the forest. While he was lost, he came upon the Meadow of the Ookees. He told the children of his time there, and of how the Fireflies guided him safely home again.

He explained to them how he kept the Ookee's secret. He never told anyone where the Ookees were, how to get there, or even admitted that there were people called Ookees. He told his parents that while he was away from home and lost, he dreamed about the little people. He never intended to invade the privacy of the Ookees again until now.

"So that's why the people in town say you are crazy, er I mean..." Joey said, stopping himself. But it was too late. He had already said something that he felt sure had insulted Anthony.

"Oh, that's okay, Joey. That is what they say. But it is my fault they say it, you know. Ifen I had only mentioned my dream to my mother and father and not keep talking about it to everyone else in the town; they would not have gotten that impression of me. Don't blame them for the way they feel.

Just remember that when you get back, say nothing to anyone else except to your mother and father. To them, tell only part of the truth. Never let them know that you were really there; and it was not just a dream. If you do, the Ookees will be discovered, or worse, you will be labeled a — Crazy, as you called it, like me." Joey and Becky laughed.

The Children listened to him talking about the Ookees for the rest of the trip home. They agreed to do the same thing as Anthony. They would keep quiet about the Ookees.

They also agreed that it would be better to just speak of the Ookees to their parents and to explain the Ookees as a dream. It would remain a secret. Even though they were young, they understood the problems that would arise if the outside world found out about the little people. The sanctity and peacefulness of the Valley would be forever ruined.

Before they knew it, they had reached the part of the stream that they had left just a few days before. It was the exact spot, where Joey had pulled his sister to the safety of the shore.

They continued to follow Anthony along the banks of the stream towards the town. They still had far to go. The sun would be up soon. They wanted to get as far as they could from Ookee Meadow. They wanted to leave the world of the Ookees as safe as possible.

The sun was starting to rise. The townspeople would soon start searching again. They had to hurry.

It wasn't long, before they began to hear many voices. The voices were coming from the townspeople who were again starting out to search for the children. They were coming up on a bend in the river. The voices seemed to be coming from just around the bend. Soon after they had rounded the curve in the stream, a few of the townspeople could be seen in the distance. Suddenly, one of the townspeople realized that there were people up ahead.

"Look! I see some people up ahead," shouted one of the men.

As they got nearer, they saw a man with two children behind him. They were walking single file and heading up stream to where they were searching. Could it be? Was it too much to hope for?

"It's the children!" one of them shouted.

"They're with Anthony," shouted another.

They had found the children. Everyone was cheering. Some were even crying with joy.

"Thank God, we've found the two of you," said the Sheriff, tears flowing from his eyes. He grabbed the two children and held them tight in his arms.

"But you didn't find us, Anthony did," said Becky.

"You're right, Becky," the Sheriff said, laughing and crying at the same time.

As he held tight to her, he was checking to see if she was all right.

"Are you hurt anywhere, Becky?" he asked.

"No, I feel just fine," she answered.

"What about Joey?" he asked.

One of the others had grabbed him up in all the excitement.

"He looks fine from what I can see," was the man's response.

"How do you feel, Joey?"

"Great, I feel just great," he said, as he smiled.

The whole town seemed to be with them now. Everyone was laughing and crying with the children as well. It was true. Anthony had found them.

"Anthony, you're a hero," called out one of the townsfolk.

"Yes, Anthony, but how?" asked a bewildered Sheriff, as he put Becky down. He was thinking more clearly.

"Oh, I guess you could say that I was just walking around checking the bushes and thickets. I kinda bumped into them."

Anthony looked down at the children and winked. Joey and Becky just smiled back and said nothing.

"But you were heading back. When did you get out here? How did you know where to search? Where were they when you found them?" Voices shouted, from every direction.

"Hey, I'm kind of hungry," interrupted Joey. He was hoping to change the subject.

"Me too. All we had was berries and…" she stopped, as Joey nudged her with his elbow, unseen by anyone else.

"All we have had were berries and spring water," Joey went on to say.

"Come on Sheriff," called out one of the men. "Let's get these kids back to their parents."

By now, the questions were forgotten. The people of the town were hurrying along the path of the bank carrying the children. They wrapped the children in the warm blankets that they had brought with them.

Everyone headed for the bridge where the terrible tragedy had started. The sun was climbing higher in the sky now and its rays brought warmth to the children's faces. As soon as they reached the street, the children wanted to get down. They wanted to go the rest of the way home by themselves.

"Hey, put us down," said Joey. He felt foolish being carried.

"Yah, me too," said Becky, as her brother was placed on the sidewalk.

"Come on Becky, let's go," Joey ordered. The two started to run for home. They had missed their parents a great deal and couldn't wait to see them again. They ran as fast as they could. They began to shout as they got closer to home.

"Mom! Dad! Mom! Dad!" the children shouted over and over again.

Joey had his sister by the hand. She had her trusty Pookie Bear clutched tightly under her arm. He was running so fast, he was almost dragging her along.

At their little modest house on the edge of town, Becky and Joey's parents were sitting on the steps. They were comforting each other that their children would soon be found and brought back to them safe and sound.

"Oh, Jonathan, they have to be all right," sobbed their mother, Peggy.

"They will. They will," answered their father, but not convincingly.

"I heard the Sheriff say if the children are not found by tomorrow, they will start dragging the lake in Boone County that the stream empties into," Peggy said, as she went on sobbing.

Jonathan could say nothing. He was filled with sorrow and anger. His children were missing, and he was unable to do anything about it. He knew that his place was here with his wife; she needed him now. The townspeople were trained to search the woods, fields and the other areas surrounding the town. Most of them had grown up here and knew the area by heart.

Suddenly, Mrs. Mitchell looked up, and was staring into space.

"What's wrong, Peggy?" he asked her.

"*Shh*," she whispered, as she covered his mouth with her hand.

"Peggy," he said, after he took her hand from his face.

She gave him no response, but covered his mouth again with her hand to stop him from talking. Again, he removed her hand and shook her lightly to get her attention. He was trying to waken her from the trance she seemed to be in.

"Please, Jonathan, be still. I thought I heard something," she replied. "Did you hear anything?" she asked her husband.

"No, not a thing," he replied.

"I thought I heard the children calling to us," she said, as she stood up. She slowly walked in the direction of the road that lay in front of their house.

"It's your mind playing tricks on you, that's all. Sit down here and wait. Give the Sheriff time to do his job."

"No, I heard them. I know I did," she said, as she started to run down their walk and into the street.

Jonathan got up and went after her.

"Joey, Becky, I hear you. I'm coming. I'm coming," she yelled, as she began running and crying at the same time.

Mr. Mitchell ran to the street, hoping to stop his wife from being disappointed. He knew that in such sad times and times of stress, folks were known to hear things, especially things they most wanted to hear.

When he got to the road, he could see in the distance the figures of two small children. They were racing up the cobblestone walk from the center of town.

His wife was now running towards them. Could it be? Was it possible? Were the children really running up the street, strong and safe and heading for her open arms, or was it just a dream? Was it just their minds playing tricks on them?

He thought all of these things in a brief second. Then, he too, started to run. He ran faster than he had ever run in his whole entire life. As he got closer to the two youngsters, he could see that they were indeed his children. They were his lost children that were now found. They were deliriously happy and were laughing. He could hear them calling now.

"Mom! Dad! Mom! Dad!" were their shouts, their cries for their parents.

"Yes, babies. It's Mommy. I'm coming. I'm coming," their mother wept, as she kept running for what seemed an eternity.

As the children and their mother met, their arms embraced each other. They sat on the ground crying, hugging, and not letting go. Mr. Mitchell had joined them. All were crying and happy.

Soon, the townsfolk had caught up. They were crying for joy right along with them.

"How did you find them? Where did you find them?" their mother asked. "Are you all right? Are either of you hurt?"

"We're fine, Mom," said Joey, as he finally let go and caught his breath.

"How did they finally find you?" she

asked in the middle of the excitement. At that moment, the Sheriff caught up with the group that was gathered there.

"We didn't," answered the sheriff. "Your neighbor did."

"What neighbor did?" asked Jonathan in shock. "Which neighbor?"

"Anthony!"

"Anthony, who is Anthony?" he asked, wiping the tears from his eyes.

"There, Anthony, your neighbor," said the Sheriff, pointing to the old man he had last seen rocking in his chair. He was the same man he had called crazy.

Now in the midst of the crowd stood Anthony, the strange old man everyone considered quite odd but harmless.

He looked at the children and at their parents with a smile on his face. Without saying a word, he walked by them, back straight and head held high. He headed back home to his porch and his rocking chair.

After some good old-fashioned crying and laughter, their parents took the children home.

Someone had alerted the town's doctor that the children had been found. He rushed right over to check on them. As soon as he arrived, he rushed the children into the bedroom.

His examination seemed to take forever. Everyone stood by, in the house and outside, awaiting his findings. Finally, after tucking them snugly in their parents' bed, he came out to talk to their mother and father.

"I have given them a good going over. I can find nothing at all wrong with them except for a few bruises here and there, from their fall from the bridge. That's to be expected. Outside of being tired, there's nothing else wrong with them, that a really good sleep won't cure," he said as he smiled. "Now, let's all get out of here and let these folks get some rest. Besides, I have some really sick people who need my attention," he said, as they all laughed.

"Now, keep in mind, Mr. and Mrs.

Mitchell, that they have been through a very traumatic experience. I have found that in cases like this, it is better not to ask questions. The children will come around and talk about what happened when they are ready. Bombarding them with questions could cause damage to them, maybe irreversible damage. Let them do the talking. Don't ask them to go into detail. The sooner they forget this terrible accident, the better it will be for them."

"All right, doctor, no questions," agreed the children's parents.

"But, I have questions for the children," said the Sheriff.

"Your questions will have wait," said the doctor, getting a little aggravated. "I'll let you know when you can talk to them. I mean that; and as I said, no questions."

The Sheriff threw his hands in the air, nodded in agreement and turned to escort the rest of the townspeople from the house.

The doctor walked over to Anthony's porch. He got there as the Sheriff and his deputies started to question Anthony.

"Come on, Anthony, let's go inside so I can check you over as well," interrupted the doctor, before Anthony had a chance to answer any of the Sheriff's questions.

"Now, wait a minute, Doc," protested the Sheriff, getting quite aggravated with him. "I listened to you and left the children alone.

Now, let me talk to Anthony before you whisk him away as well, will ya?"

The doctor ignored the Sheriff, as if he wasn't even there.

"Dang that Doc," the Sheriff said, as he took his hat off and threw it on the ground.

Inside the doctor sat across from Anthony in the sitting room. He was not examining him, only staring at him.

"Everything all right with you, Anthony?" the doctor asked.

"Just fine, just fine," was Anthony's only reply.

"Thought I'd get you out of there before the questions started," the doctor said.

"Let them ask their questions. What kinda answers do you think they will get from a crazy man?" Anthony replied, as the two of them laughed, as if they both knew what had happened without talking about it.

The children kept their promise and only spoke of the Ookees as a dream. They spent much of their leisure time with their new friend, Anthony. They would spend hours talking about their adventures with the inhabitants of Fantasy Valley.

Mr. and Mrs. Mitchell never said anything about, what Anthony had said to them about the little people. They felt a strong bond with Anthony now. They felt that it was better to forget all about that conversation. They never discussed it, and yet they never forgot the words that their neighbor had said.

They never asked questions when the

children told them, that they had had a dream about the Little People. Yes, the children had been safe with the little people, the little people of Ookee Village, of Ookee Meadow, of the place that existed in Fantasy Valley.

THE END

Of the BEGINNING